"Watching you...seeing your pleasure...is exciting..."

"You're prejudiced," Sam teased as she sprawled beside Matt on the couch.

"Yep."

They were quiet for a moment. Watching the tape of themselves avidly. It wasn't the kind of sex that was scandalous. It was slow. No music. But it was raw and exciting. The feeling of being inside Sam swept over Matt, making his belly clench. It was a little crazy considering what he'd just figured out.

He touched her cheek, wondering if she was seeing the same thing he was. They weren't just having sex. They were making love.

By all rights the realization should've scared the hell out of him.

"This makes me want you all over again," he whispered, pulling her onto his lap.

Her voice became husky. "Prove it..."

Dear Reader,

Welcome back to the Three Wicked Nights trilogy! Finally, I get to write Sam's book. She's the one who designed the smart apartment. The one the guys looked after when she was at MIT. Only, not all of her college heroes have given the apartment a trial run.

In fact, the only one she's lost touch with is Matt Wilkinson, the heir apparent to the Wilkinson family. Matt has large shoes to fill as he rises up the corporate ladder, but a short trip to Boston changes things.

He surprises his old friend Samantha, who lends him the smart apartment, but she's freaked out by his arrival! Doesn't he know that she had a crush on him for far too long?

Matt isn't just coming to catch up with Sam. He wants to make amends for something he'd done in the past. Something that he's never forgiven himself for.

What neither of them counted on was that the spark between the old friends lights up like a beacon from the moment they see each other. Only this time it's not a girlish crush Sam has, but a full-on case of unrequited love.

I had a great time writing this book. Matt is one of my all-time favorite heroes, and I hope you fall in love with him just like I did.

You can find me at jomk.tumblr.com. Come on by and drop me a note!

Take care,

Jo Leigh

Jo Leigh

One Blazing Night

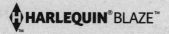

Recycling programs
for this product may
not exist in your area.

ISBN-13: 978-0-373-79891-9

One Blazing Night

Copyright © 2016 by Jolie Kramer

Printed in U.S.A.

www.Harlequin.com

Jo Leigh is from Los Angeles and always thought she'd end up living in Manhattan. So how did she end up in Utah in a tiny town with a terrible internet connection, being bossed around by a houseful of rescued cats and dogs? What the heck, she says, predictability is boring. Jo has written more than forty-five novels for Harlequin. Visit her website at joleigh.com or contact her at joleigh@joleigh.com.

Books by Jo Leigh

Harlequin Blaze

Ms. Match
Sexy Ms. Takes
Shiver
Hotshot
Lying in Bed
All the Right Moves

Three Wicked Nights

One Breathless Night
One Sizzling Night
One Blazing Night

It's Trading Men

Choose Me
Have Me
Want Me
Seduce Me
Dare Me
Intrigue Me

To get the inside scoop on Harlequin Blaze and its talented writers, be sure to check out BlazeAuthors.com.

All backlist available in ebook format.

Visit the Author Profile page at Harlequin.com for more titles.

To my friends Jill Shalvis and Debbi Rawlins and my wonderful editor, Birgit Davis-Todd.

1

As the music from her headphones blasted the sound track from *Raiders of the Lost Ark*, Samantha O'Connel narrowed her eyes in her attempt to read a note left by her newest part-time employee, Tina Albert. Tina was an MIT student, just like the other six people Sam employed at her company, SOC Electronics. Tina was cute, bright, witty, completely dedicated to doing a good job. And she had terrible handwriting.

It wasn't her fault, really. By the time Tina was born, there were millions of teenagers who hardly ever needed to write. They came of age at the dawn of smartphones. But Tina would have to learn to write more clearly.

Sam rubbed her eyes and took another look. Maybe she could have read the chicken scratches if she hadn't worked until midnight. She'd skipped dinner and hadn't looked up until just past midnight. Again.

She was getting old. At twenty, sleep had been optional, but at twenty-nine, there were only so many nights she could get five hours and feel refreshed the next day. She certainly needed to be alert.

Ah. The note was a reminder that the new hard drive

had been delivered to the smart apartment. Sam didn't have time to install it and wouldn't for at least a week. Neither would Clark, though she wouldn't have asked him to anyway. The prototype apartment was her baby—she'd bought the building in Boston's Financial District with her personal money and designed all the electronics herself. Luckily, the new drive wasn't actually necessary for the apartment to function, but it would help with the intermittent sensor problems she'd noted on her logs.

So far, the apartment was a raging success but needed some refinements. No paying guests had stayed there yet, only her friends and family. Each one had given her a critique and made suggestions—some of them really good—but she was too busy for a hobby that was so complex. Sadly, that was the only kind of hobby she liked. Well, except for gaming. Which was more part of her DNA than a hobby.

Clark, who'd been her assistant since her senior year at MIT, had told her they needed to hire people to help with administrative duties, man the booths at trade shows, and more important, take over some of the testing of new parts and equipment, the writing of instruction manuals and the handling of customer support lines. Which meant whomever they hired had a steep learning curve from day one.

She'd always hated delegating, but when Clark pointed out the new employees would be taking over things both of them hated to do, she'd jumped all over it. With the exception of Tina, the students all worked on the second floor, under Clark's supervision, so that Sam had minimal contact with them.

It wasn't that she was a snob; she just wasn't the most social person. She'd started working on her own in high school, and with one notable exception, her solo work habits had solidified at MIT. By the time she'd graduated, she'd decided, against her parents' firm objections, not to accept the invitations to join Google or Apple or Microsoft and to just do what she liked. So she'd started SOC Electronics—not only her initials, but also the acronym of a computer miracle device called the System On Chip, which integrated all the components of a computer into a single chip.

She'd become a corporation before she'd turned twenty. It had been difficult to work with Clark in the beginning, but now he was like another pair of her own hands. In the end, Sam was in charge of the tech creation and problem solving. Clark was in charge of the rest. Tina was a one-off. She was really smart, but dammit, she was still afraid to jump in during brainstorming sessions.

Sam sighed. She was probably being too harsh on the girl. Tina had a lot of potential, and in time, Sam believed she'd turn out to be a real asset. If Sam had got enough sleep last night, she probably wouldn't be feeling so cranky.

Lesson? For God's sake, go to sleep at a sane hour even if it meant not completing a drawing or leaving a task for the next day.

She grabbed her phone and set the alarm. At eight o'clock she'd stop working, no matter what. Then she'd make sure she was asleep by eleven.

Her cell phone flashed with a new call, making her jerk as if she'd been slapped. It was only Clark getting her attention. After pulling out her right earbud, she turned to find him coming from the clean room at the back of the building.

By the time he'd passed the computers and large schematics workstations occupying the middle of the workshop, he'd pulled off his clean-room whites, leaving him in his regular jeans and T-shirt. "I'm doing a run to the stationery store after lunch. If you want anything—"

"Yes." She swiveled her chair so she could look straight at him. Her gaze caught on the nifty new 3-D resin printer that she couldn't even play with until this job was done. Tina was going to learn everything there was to know about the machine so she could show Sam how to use it. "I need more mechanical pencils."

"Already? You do know that most people don't use a pencil a day, right? What am I saying. You want more pencils, I'll get them for you. Anything else?"

She winced but said it anyway, as quickly as she could. "A combo falafel-and-shawarma plate with a side of baba ghanoush?"

Clark gave her a very judgey look. "Sam. It's almost lunchtime. Do you have any idea how long it's going to take me to find a parking spot?"

"We could send Tina."

"Tina isn't here this morning. Remember? Dentist. She has a thing about Novocain… Never mind."

Sam almost suggested sending someone from upstairs, but she was sidelined by Clark's comment. He knew Tina had a thing about Novocain? Huh. Clark often talked about the troops, but this was a new level of detail. "Admit it," she said as she smiled. "You want a falafel, too, don't you?"

He looked very put-upon even though it was more out of habit than any real issue. He really was the safest human she knew. It helped that he had no interest whatsoever in her social life.

"Yes," he said. "Dammit. You're evil. And you have to call in the orders. But you're still evil. A pox upon thee."

"Oh, my...you had the D&D tournament last night, didn't you? It must have gone well or you'd have already bitched to me about it."

"I'm still in."

"Cool. Watch out for that guy, the blond with the—" She wiggled her fingers near her ear. She hated those big black plugs in the middle of the lobe. They made her skin crawl.

"Oh, he's out. He's out so far he has to wear an oxygen tank."

"Well played, Dark Mage of Harrow Glen."

He bowed, then took off his bootees, but that didn't make his courtly gesture any less goofy. Hell, she was just as bad. Her love of computer games and the cosplay that came with it had been the genesis of her whole career, one that was more successful than she could have ever predicted.

In the past four years, she'd revolutionized spyware with her new sensor technology and signed a multimillion-dollar contract with the US Department of Defense. But it was her coding skills and the development of two different antihacking programs that had brought in the big money. She rarely thought about that, though. She was happy with her little house and her huge lab. They were on adjoining plots of land in Bay Village, and being so close to the heart of downtown Boston made everything so simple. That she was a wealthy entrepreneur felt so discordant with the image she held of herself. Truth was, she was happiest playing "Ms. Pac-Man" on the vintage arcade machine she kept in her living room.

As Clark raided the petty cash for lunch money, she called in their orders. The Falafel King was number seven on the speed dial. What did that say about her life? Nothing she wanted to think about now. After ordering, she went to her drafting table and took another look at the schematics for the nano drive she'd been working on. The temperature issue was fixed—sort of. It would mean the buyers would have to build special cold rooms that had to be so safe they'd stand up to the end of the world. But that wasn't the problem she was working on today.

After putting her earbud in once more, letting her classical music light up her brain, she put her cell phone close enough that she'd notice if Clark called again. Then Sam began her review of the design in her usual way, starting wherever her eyes fell, usually somewhere in the middle. God, how her technique had driven her professors insane.

Something occurred to her—a bright shiny idea that might just solve an issue she'd shoved to the back of her mind, and then she was in the zone.

At the worst possible time, she caught her cell phone flashing. "Clark," she muttered as she ripped out her right earbud and answered. "What?"

"Huh. That's one way to answer the phone."

It wasn't—

But it couldn't be—

Matthew Wilkinson. Matt? *Matt!*

Sam hadn't heard his voice in a very long time.

Her eyes shut tight as the world stopped turning. As the memories piled one on top of another. He was her first. Her very, very first love. And her first heartbreak.

She wasn't sure how long she'd been dancing on the head of a pin, but surely he must have thought she'd fainted or something. Well, *something* had definitely happened— most of her major organs were spinning around like tops.

Matt had been one of her best friends back in her MIT days. She'd been fourteen as a freshman, so all her friends had been four or five years older—and they'd all happened to be guys. They'd bonded over gaming, Marvel comics and bad horror movies. And none of them had been bothered by her age. The guys had protected her. Teased her. And they hadn't cared that she had the social skills of a paper clip.

"Hello? Still there?"

"Hu…hi, Matt?"

"You okay?"

"Just dropped my pencil," she said, gripping the phone so tightly she thought it might break. "Sorry."

"I know it's been forever. How are you, Sammy?" he asked, his voice dipping lower in a way that made her melt.

No one called her Sammy. She hadn't heard that name in so long she'd figured she'd never hear it again. It made her blush, and she was grateful there was nobody there to see her. She needed to get off the phone. She couldn't think. There was too much going on in her head and she'd already started doodling, which wasn't helping. All she needed to do was tell him she'd call him back. "I'm… I'm…fine. I'm good. Better."

"Better? Was something wrong?"

"No. Not as such. No. Just— That would be no. Nothing was wrong. I meant to say 'richer.'"

He laughed. "I'd kind of figured that after reading about your work. So you weren't quite as dim as we all led you to believe, huh?"

"Not quite." Her face was so hot she was reasonably sure she was going to burst into flames any second. She was a jumble of emotions. It wasn't fair, him calling her out of the blue. It had taken her so long to get over him, after all. "How are you?" she asked, trying to keep her voice cheerful.

That should buy her a couple of minutes. But she needed to listen. What if he said he was dying or something and she missed it?

"I'm good. Jet-lagged. Just got in from Tokyo."

"Godzilla stirring up trouble again?"

"I wish," he said, his voice the same. Exactly the same. She wanted to curl up under the covers and dream about him for a week. "Nothing but boring contracts to negotiate."

"But you still like being a lawyer, right?"

"Some days are better than others. But yeah."

"And you're living in New York?" Was she supposed to know that was where he lived? Oh, God. Why was she still talking?

"I am," he said, the words delivering both disappointment and relief. If he'd moved back to Boston, she would've died. "Hey, I heard from Logan last night."

Logan was part of the gang that had always had her back in college. "I saw him in June," she said, thankful for the safe shift in conversation.

"Yeah, I know. He said that crazy apartment of yours is not to be missed. I'm a little hurt that I wasn't invited for a test run."

Hi there, worst nightmare! She held back the groan that had come with the thought. "We haven't talked since you... For a long time. I wasn't sure..."

"That's true," he said, rescuing her as he'd done so often when her words got stuck. Then he sighed. "I want to blame it on traveling the way I do. And my marriage. Or my divorce. Pick one, and it'll be true. Bottom line? I've thought about you. Especially when I've happened to catch yet another article about some new, brilliant thing you've invented. To be honest, I figured you'd probably only answer the phone for Stephen Hawking, not guys like me."

"Not a guy like you? I talk to Logan and Rick. They're not Hawking. I don't even know Stephen Hawking. He never calls."

"Never writes? Bastard."

She smiled and some of her parts relaxed. Not her heart, though. That was still doing cartwheels even as she tried to put on the brakes. "I'm still me," she said, as a reminder to herself more than him. "Still can't talk on the phone worth a damn. Still watching my old copies of *Robot Chicken* and playing 'World of Warcraft.'"

"Thank God," he said. "I'd hate it if you weren't you. No, that's wrong. We all change, and I'm sure you have, too. You're certainly doing a great job in the career department."

"I have people. Lawyers. A financial planner and a business manager. They talk business. I talk to tech people, so that's like school."

"I'm glad. I really am. Look, I'm coming to Boston for a week or so, and I'd love to stay in that smart apartment, at least for a few days. But mostly, I want to see you."

See her? Why? "Okay," she said, because she was an idiot and she couldn't think straight and this was Matt. "When are you coming?"

"In three days."

"Oh. Wow. I'm not exactly sure of the schedule, so when Clark gets back, I'll have him check, okay? He usually makes things, um, happen, so, you know, he's at lunch but he'll give you a call."

After a tense pause, Matt said, "I will get to see you, right?"

No. The word she was looking for was *no*. She couldn't see him. Not in a million years. It would be a disaster of epic proportions. "Yeah. Of course. I've got some deadline things, but, you know."

He laughed. Quietly. Fondly. And that was the stuff that made him so dangerous. He was rich, gorgeous, smart as a whip and could have any woman on the planet. And he was her friend. The problem was that she'd fallen in love with him two minutes after midnight on her sixteenth birthday and now it was all too clear she hadn't let go of that silly pipe dream. Great. This couldn't suck more.

"I'm glad Clark is still there with you."

"Yeah. Couldn't do it without him. But he also does some cool stuff on his own."

After a brief silence that proved to Sam it was impossible to swallow with a dry mouth, Matt said, "I'm excited to see you, Sammy."

"I'm wearing a *Black Widow* sweatshirt and black tights I bought at a flea market in Cambridge."

"Okay. Wait. Didn't you used to wear something like that back at MIT?"

"Yep. Same sweatshirt."

"That's my girl." This time Matt's laugh put her on edge. She felt like that socially inept teenager he'd befriended a lifetime ago. "Okay, I'll let you get back to work," he said. "Let me know about the apartment."

"Will do."

After they disconnected, she put her cell phone back where it belonged, picked up her iPod and changed the music to Led Zeppelin.

The pounding drumbeat synced to her thudding heart. She couldn't see him. She couldn't. God. But what if…?

MATT DRANK IN the sight of the New York City skyline, and as always, he lingered on the Chrysler Building, his favorite. It was a clear fall night, and from his twenty-fourth-floor penthouse, everything looked the way it did in the movies. His trip to Asia had lasted two long months but was well worth it. He'd negotiated a nice purchase price for an international hotel chain, Voyager Hotels. It was a big win for Wilkinson Holdings and for him personally. He needed all the points he could get with the board meeting coming up. It was time for him to take the next step up the ladder, which meant taking charge of the London office. Since WH was a family business—his family's—there were people on the board who believed every victory of his was somehow manipulated by his father and two uncles.

Even with all the politics that came with being in-house counsel for a top-100 company, he wouldn't change anything. Well, except for that London gig. He wanted that. Enough to play the game the way his father had taught him.

But right now it felt great to be home. It also felt great to be alone. He needed to relax for the next couple of days, get over the jet lag before he went to Boston and made nice at the corporate office. The company's annual gala for the Boston Children's Hospital was coming up—a great cause but always a chore. Two days after the fund-raiser was the annual board meeting.

He'd much rather think about his upcoming mini vacation. Although Boston was really home. He'd been born and raised in Beacon Hill. Gone to two universities in Cambridge, had a lot of friends who lived in the city.

The only one he cared to see this time was Sam. She'd been on his mind since he'd heard from his buddy Logan McCabe. He and Logan both lived in New York but rarely saw each other, with Matt's crazy travel schedule. But as soon as Logan had told him about the smart apartment and Sam, that was it. Matt had picked up the phone and she'd answered, and it was like going back in time.

She was terrible on the phone. Always had been. But it had been great to hear her voice. Logan had said she'd stepped up her game when it came to the business and was still a workaholic. Matt had known from their first few conversations at MIT that she was going to play in the big leagues one day.

He'd seen a couple of pictures of her online, neither of which had been very good. It seemed she was still camera shy, mainly because of her freckles, he imagined. She'd always hated them. There was just a spray of them across her nose, but she thought they made her look hideous. That and her copper penny–red hair.

She'd tried dyeing it black once. What a nightmare that had been. Goth and Sam did not go together. She was far too earnest and far too sensible to fall in with a crowd that demanded such conformity. Eventually, her hair had grown out and the nose ring had disappeared. He wondered if she still had that row of piercings climbing up the outer shell of her left ear.

Damn, he was anxious to see her. After he'd graduated and moved out of the house the gang had shared off campus, he hadn't spoken to Sam but for a couple of times. Then he'd started law school and she was working on her second master's, and with their hectic schedules the communication had dwindled to a few texts here and there, mostly around the holidays and special occasions. Once he'd married Vanessa, he and Sam had stopped texting.

He wasn't sure why, but for his part it had felt like the right thing to do, even though Sam wasn't a romantic interest. Hell, she was five years younger than he was and so much smarter that there was no chart for it. Not that he was a lightweight, because goddamn *Harvard Law Review* his second year. But she was made of different stuff.

Back at MIT they'd bonded over computer games and insomnia, right along with Logan and Rick, who'd also lived at Randall Hall, and the four of them had become thick as thieves. They had all felt somewhat protective of Sam. She might have been smart enough to take on Hawking, but she hadn't been quite old enough to navigate university life on her own. So the guys had kept their eye on her in the dorm and had even run interference a few times on campus. One particular incident still made him wince and smile at the same time. It had ended with him getting a hell of a shiner.

Sometimes he'd wondered if Sam felt that talking to him, to the three of them, was like talking to a pet. She'd never implied that she felt she was intellectually above them, but none of the rest of them had been able to understand the complexity of her studies. They hadn't had to. They hadn't cared about her grades, her habits, any of that. The four of them had laughed a lot. Watched a lot of weird movies. Played a lot of computer games. She always said they made her feel normal. Well, normal-ish.

He couldn't wait to see her.

He'd had a beer with dinner, but now it was time for a little Johnnie Walker Black. Nightcap of champions.

Matt's bones ached and he had that plane smell on

him. He'd let the scotch settle him down, have a long hot shower, then hit the sheets.

But as he sipped his drink, another memory, not a great one, stirred. Like so many college kids, he'd done his share of foolish things, made a few reckless choices, engaged in some risky behavior that would've stunned anyone who knew him now. He wasn't proud of any of it, but that night long ago when he'd messed up with Sam was the worst. The truth was, things had changed after that. He'd learned a lot about the wisdom of sobriety that night. That was all in the past, though, and now he'd have a chance to get to know her again. At least, he hoped so. She'd sounded a little reluctant. But then, with Sam it was hard to tell for sure. He'd forgotten just how much she disliked talking on the phone.

Picturing her with the stupid nose ring, he smiled. Seeing her again and catching up was going to be pure, uncomplicated fun.

2

SAM LEANED AGAINST the wall, staring out the window of the smart apartment from an angle so Matt couldn't see her when he finally arrived.

If he arrived. But of course he was coming, because he'd said so. She'd hate to think she'd gone through the crazy whirlwind of deciding what to wear for nothing. Good Lord, she must've tried on everything in her closet, avoiding the sweatshirts, T-shirts and leggings that made up most of her wardrobe. She wanted to look good for Matt. But the few dresses she owned for wearing to conferences and business meetings made her feel like an impostor when she put them on.

So Sam had compromised. Business slacks with her nicest San Diego Comic-Con T-shirt. She'd had the shirt for a long time, but it would be new to Matt. It was blue with long sleeves. She'd tried pushing those up, but her arm freckles made the decision to wear them down very easy. Still, it was a good hair day and she was thankful for small favors.

Now it was all she could do not to run back home and

put on a sweatshirt and leggings. What had she been thinking?

Ha. As if she didn't know. Matt was coming. Today. Any minute. So she could give him the key. Which meant she'd slept like shit. When Clark had offered to give him the key, she'd immediately said no. He'd seemed agitated. Probably because it meant she wouldn't be working. But screw it. SOC was her company, and she could take a few hours off if she wanted to.

Or maybe Clark wasn't piqued because she wouldn't be working but because of *why* she wouldn't be working. Did he not like Matt? Huh. She'd have to think about that. Was it because she'd worn her dress pants? Did Clark think she was selling out? Trying to be someone she wasn't? The fact that she turned into an idiot when she was around Matt wasn't anything new in her life, and Clark had no doubt caught on. Her crush had lasted a really long time.

Clark might be upset at her foolishness, and she couldn't fault his logic. Especially when she considered that Matt wouldn't care what she wore.

She shouldn't have cared, either. But she had the feeling Matt would look spiffy and handsome as hell and she hadn't wanted to— Something caught her eye at the window. Oh, God. *Matt.* He was here. Getting out of a taxi—

Not a town car. Most of his family lived here. Their corporate office was located downtown. She hadn't expected a taxi.

Or for her reaction to be this bad.

How had her mouth already dried up? Her heart had been pounding since she'd seen him in her peripheral vision. For heaven's sake, butterflies and panic were battling to the death in her chest. Why hadn't she just let Clark give him the damn key?

Matt was taking his time. Checking out the brownstones that lined the street before taking the shady brick walkway that led to the apartment. He looked like her Matt, but different, too. Broader of chest, certainly. He seemed taller, but she doubted that was true. Maybe his black jeans and gray V-neck sweater made him appear taller than the six foot one she knew he was. His jacket was dark, maybe suede, and looked as if it would be nice to curl up against.

Not that she would be curling up against anyone.

Even his luggage looked sharp. And—wow—he'd brought a lot. An extra-large suitcase on wheels and a brown garment bag. Was he planning to stay until winter?

Just as he was reaching the front door, she realized she'd been squeezing the key so hard it had left a deep groove in her hand. The hand he'd want to shake. No, he'd want a hug.

She hadn't considered—

The sound of the doorbell made her jump. Oh, this was going to be a load of fun. Why was she stressing so much? This was Matt. They were practically brother and sister. Except for that one time… Shit. Why did she have to think of that?

She needed to concentrate on breathing. And trying not to pass out. After a long, deep breath, she squared her shoulders and opened the door.

Holy crap. Matt's brown eyes and perfectly shaped mouth were the same, yet he was so much better-looking than she'd remembered. A man now, not a boy. And the smile he gave her sent shivers through her body. She knew that grin. It changed his face. He could look really serious and foreboding if he wanted to, but when he whipped out that grin, he became a tease, a wink, a promise.

"Wow," he said, his voice lower, maybe not. "You look great."

"Me?" She pointed at him. "You—"

"Look the same, just old." He paused, waited. "Mind if I come in?"

"Of course." She quickly stood aside. And she wasn't disappointed that there'd been no hug. Hugs were overdone. They hadn't seen each other for years. She closed the door, focusing on the image of his smile, even as she understood it would haunt her dreams for ages.

MATT LEFT HIS LUGGAGE off to the side and watched Sam turn in her Comic-Con shirt, with her copper-colored hair shifting over her shoulders. She was a woman now, beautifully sculpted with curves that hadn't been there when he'd last seen her. But that shirt? That was pure Sammy.

He couldn't get over it. The pictures online hadn't done her justice at all. She didn't have prom-queen beauty— that wasn't Sam. She could stand to put on a couple of pounds and her smile was a little crooked, but she had amazing green eyes that lit up like firecrackers. Standing there in front of him was everything he'd always liked about Sammy, with the addition of womanly grace that only time and experience could bring.

He couldn't wait another moment. "Come here," he said, holding his arms out, taking the first step.

A blush stole over her cheeks but she came willingly, and then she was in his arms. A second later, hers went around his waist, under his jacket.

It wasn't the MIT hug he was used to.

They'd never pressed this close, never hung on for beat after beat of his quickening heart. Damn, she smelled good.

He pulled back. She released him instantly, but he wasn't quite ready to abandon ship. He held on to her shoulders and gave her a head-to-toe inspection.

"Logan was right. You've turned into a stunner."

Her brows, a little darker than her hair, came together as she frowned and took a half step back. "You don't have to say that stuff to me, Matt. I don't need to be flattered."

"You think I wasn't being sincere?"

"No. I mean, I know I'm okay. But I'm not— I'm in shape because I think better when I'm running. It's not about…anything else."

"I'm glad you're fit, but I wasn't lying. I think you're beautiful, and that's just the truth."

"Okay," she said as the blush darkened. "That's fair enough. I think you're beautiful, too."

He laughed. "I think the word you were looking for was *handsome*? I hope?"

"Fine. Handsome. Hot as hell. Drop-dead gorgeous. Mouthwatering—"

"Okay. That's enough." Matt laughed, mostly at himself. How could he have forgotten her quirky tendency to drive them all nuts with the thesaurus in her brain. "Hey," he said, giving her another once-over. "You're taller. By a lot. When did that happen?"

Sam looked confused and then dropped her gaze to her toes, peeking out from under the hem of her slacks. "I'm wearing heels," she said and then lifted her right leg to show him the proof. "Anyway…" She stuck out her hand. The key rested in her palm. "Here's the key."

Matt accepted it, wondering why she suddenly seemed so nervous.

She moved back and turned in a jerky motion. "This is it," she said, gesturing widely. "It's still a prototype. I'm working out the kinks." She took off walking down the hall and he lagged a few seconds behind until she reached the junction of kitchen and living room. "The fridge and pantry are fully stocked. Feel free to use or consume anything."

She picked up some brochure from the kitchen counter. "You'll find everything you need in here, including chefs who will come here to cook or have something made-to-order delivered. The masseur is terrific, especially his sports massage. I know you know Boston, but there are a bunch of delivery menus by the pantry. And if you have any problems or questions—"

"You've used this masseur?"

"What?" Sam frowned. "Of course not."

"You said he was terrific."

"I could find out which doctor you should use if you had an enlarged prostate. It doesn't mean I have personal experience."

Matt let out a laugh. He'd missed this. She never had thought like everyone else. Thank goodness that hadn't changed. "Point taken."

"As I was saying, if you have any questions, just call the office. Clark knows this place inside and out."

Confused, he looked down at the brochure she'd shoved into his hand. When he lifted his gaze again, he realized she was about to leave. Three steps away, he nabbed her wrist. "What? Where are you going? I want you to show me around, not give me some brochure."

"I should get back to work," she said. "Besides, Rick

and Logan didn't need me to hold their hands, and they did fine."

"Tough. They didn't have to beg for an invitation, either. So now, Sammy, my friend, you get to show me where I'll be staying for the next few days."

She glanced over her shoulder. "You have a lot of luggage for a few days."

"You know corporate is here. I've got the annual dog and pony show to attend."

"So why didn't you leave your stuff at the office?"

"I came straight from the airport."

"Really?"

He realized he'd been absently stroking her wrist when he felt her pulse leap. She pulled her arm back and he let go.

"Half an hour," he said. "That's not too bad. Right? Then you can go back to work."

She closed her eyes, her long lashes brushing the tops of her smooth pink cheeks. "Fine," she said, as if he'd asked her for a huge favor. "First lesson." Turning to face the living room wall, she said, "Call Clark."

Instantly, a monitor graphic appeared on the wall just to the right of the curved big-screen TV. The monitor was done so well it was difficult to believe it wasn't three-dimensional.

"Yeah?" Clark's voice was clear and irritated sounding as Clark removed his glasses and squinted at them. The guy looked almost the same as he had back at MIT.

"I'll be a half hour longer than I planned."

"Okay."

"I don't have any appointments, right?"

"Right. But don't tell me you're going to make it up

later, because you really have to get some sleep. Pop a Xanax, do some yoga. Whatever it takes."

"Fine. I'll drug myself to sleep tonight."

"Good." Clark's gaze shifted and he gave Matt a brief nod, then turned to Sam. "I've got that thing I'm working on," he said, pointing at his desk.

"Go," she said. "End call."

Matt got the impression Clark didn't like that Matt was keeping her from work. "I was going to say hey."

"Next time. Jeez. He's worse than my mother. Who loves him to death, of course."

"I think that was the most I ever heard him talk. But you guys are cool, right?"

"Yes," she said, the hesitation clear in her voice. "We're a finely tuned machine. We just got a new assistant, Tina. She's bright but still learning."

Matt's mind lingered on the other man. "Anything happening with you and Clark?"

"What do you mean?"

"Is it all about work, or is there something romantic—"

"With Clark?" Sam's eyes widened. "Ew. No. He's like a brother."

"Just asking." Pleased with her reaction, Matt smiled. Although, what did he care? He liked Clark, and if he and Sam had hooked up, it would've been a good thing. So what the hell—

"Do you want a tour or not?"

"Lead on."

"So, this is the living room. If you want a fire, just tell it to turn on, and it will. You can use any wall in the house for a call, but be careful. Someone accidentally made a call from the shower, so..."

He hadn't expected her to stop walking, and they

nearly collided. He put a steadying hand at the small of her back.

She jumped at the contact, then stiffened. "Sorry," she murmured.

"My fault," he said. "You okay?" She nodded and visibly relaxed. He lowered his hand, distracted by what was happening around them. The walls on either side of the fireplace had turned from white to violet. When he turned around, he realized the walls in the foyer were also shades of purple. It was fascinating. "Is that your technology?"

"The colors? Yeah. It's in all the rooms."

"What determines the color change?"

She cleared her throat. "The walls contain sensors that read the temperature of the person or people in the room. The sensors also pick up a lot of other things, like breathing and walking patterns, tonal qualities. They still need some refinement, but almost all the gizmos here do."

"That's incredible." Matt turned slowly, taking everything in. "I can already see how effective these kinds of walls could be. In high-risk situations, in hospitals—heck, in homes and hotels. This is a big deal, Sammy. Same with the monitors. The potential is unlimited."

"They're all just prototypes. But you've probably stayed in some of the best hotels in the world. You'll let me know how this compares, yes?"

He nodded as she led him into the high-end kitchen for a second time. He found himself only half listening as she explained something about ordering food, but he figured it didn't matter—he had the brochure; he'd figure it out. He wasn't here for the whiz-bang stuff, except for the fact that Sammy designed it.

It was clear this place made her tremendously happy.

Those green eyes of hers glowed with beautiful intensity. She spoke faster, too, when she was describing the apartment's amenities. Sometimes skipping words, then going back to chase them down. He loved every second of it.

The technical stuff was utterly lost on him. But this was Sammy, the girl he remembered. The heels were unexpected, though. He knew she hated them. In fact, he could only remember her wearing them twice, and both times she'd taken them off at inappropriate times. Once, she'd been in the dean's office with some big-money alumni. Matt hadn't been there, but she'd told him that halfway through explaining her thesis, her feet had started killing her, so she'd taken off her heels and put them on the dean's desk. She'd shrugged and wondered why he'd been bent out of shape about it. The alumni had handed over a major check, which was what she had been there for...

Now she was walking him to the bedroom, and the walls were turning from violet to something much darker. When they entered the bedroom itself, the colors started climbing the wall, swirling as if there were smoke in the paint, or whatever it was.

"Oh, crap," Sam said. "I forgot something." She turned around and walked past him as if the apartment were on fire.

He followed her back down the hall. "What's going on?"

"Nothing. Everything's fine. You can take your bags to your room if you want. I'll just be a minute."

"Should I be worried?"

The walls in the hallway had turned scarlet, and there was something about them that made him kind of... aroused. Not what he wanted to be. The two of them weren't like that. If she caught him with a pup tent, he was not going to be happy.

"You don't need to follow me," she muttered over her shoulder.

"Just hold on a second, will you? Tell me what's going on."

"Your bag. In your room," she said. "Now would be good."

Completely baffled, he stopped and watched her enter the kitchen and walk to the pantry. She opened the door, stepped inside, then closed the door behind her.

"What, you need a cookie?"

"Go put your bag away," she said, her muffled voice sounding stressed.

"Are you sick? You can tell me."

"Matthew. Go. Away."

"Fine," he said as he wandered into the living room and waited by a glass table that sat in front of the couch. It was the perfect vantage point, putting the pantry door in his line of sight without his crowding her. There was a small fountain trickling away somewhere, which was very pleasant, but he only had eyes for the pantry. He noticed, as he stared, that the room smelled really good. Was that what was making him horny? He was pretty damn controlled about these things, but after a few minutes of deep focus, he started to wilt.

Maybe it wasn't the smell. The color of the walls, then? But why would she want him to get worked up? The idea didn't bother him nearly as much as it should have, but it still made no sense.

The minutes ticked by and he considered getting his bags and putting them in the bedroom, but no. He was going to wait for her. If she was sick, he wanted to be

available. Although a person about to be sick would usually head to the bathroom, but then, Sammy had always
walked her own unique path.

The walls went white. All of them, all at once. It was
highly dramatic. And a little scary. "Sam?"

3

SAM EXITED THE PROGRAM and tucked her phone in her pocket. She hoped that took care of the damn mood sensors. Except now it was totally dark.

Oh, right. She opened the door.

Matt's bags were still in the foyer. He was standing near the entrance to the kitchen and was staring at her as if he expected her to say something. Only she wasn't sure what that thing was.

Matt spoke first. "Is everything okay?"

"Yes. Why wouldn't it be?" She glanced around her, trying to pretend her being in the pantry with the door closed was no big deal.

Matt walked straight past her, stepped inside the pantry, looked around and then came out a minute later carrying a box of gingersnaps.

She should have gone to the bathroom. Obviously. Why had she headed for the *pantry*, of all places? "It was just work stuff. The wall-color program wasn't working right."

"I see," he said, opening the box of cookies and holding it out to her.

She grabbed a few, knowing she was still blushing. Not a thing she could do about that. Maybe she should just wear blush-colored makeup. Huh. That way he'd never know when she was really blushing. "Anyway," she said, still chewing the little piece of cookie she'd bitten off.

"Have dinner with me?"

Her mouth stilled along with her brain. "What?"

"Dinner. With me."

"I have to go back to work. I have a deadline to meet."

"Okay. How about I get takeout from one of your many menus and bring it to your lab? I'd love to see it. I wouldn't stay long. Just enough for a quick tour and a quicker dinner."

"No," she said, her heart taking it up a notch. "I really have to work."

"I understand, but you also have to eat." He captured her hand and pulled her close.

Her hand, the one without the cookies, went right to his chest. For a moment, she froze. Just being this close to him was amazing... Smelling his wonderful scent, parts of her touching parts of him. She leaned back to look at him, to try to figure out what was going on. And met his gaze. His warm brown eyes. The eyes she'd known so well she had seen them in her sleep. "What are you doing?"

"You've filled out nicely," he said, tightening his arm around her, "but I bet you're still skipping meals. It's not a good habit, Sammy. And I don't want to play a part in it. Tonight that means you're eating with me one way or another."

Sam's mouth opened but nothing came out. She felt more confused than anything. Part of her wanted to melt into a puddle. Because he was flirting? Was that what he was doing? That was the problem. She didn't know. Not with Matt. Any other man who got this close, she would've been able to read.

But one thing was for sure—her heart rarely beat this fast. Even if he was just being nice, there was a fair chance she was going to hyperventilate.

Or she might just throw her arms around his neck and hang on forever. Years' worth of fantasies didn't just disappear because she'd forced herself to move on.

She pushed against his hard chest. "How come you're not bothering your family instead of me?"

Matt let her go so quickly she had to take a step back. "Hey, I'm sorry, Sammy. I didn't mean to—"

"Stop. You didn't." Her heart hurt at his wounded look, and she wished she could take the words back. She felt like a fool, a terrible fool, for making him feel bad when she knew better. He was just being nice. "Fine," she said, knowing it was a mistake. "We'll eat. Somehow. Together."

"Wait. Will that mean you'll have to work until some god-awful hour?"

He had a point.

She looked down and gasped a little when she saw her hand was still on his chest. He'd let her go, but she hadn't followed suit.

She smiled in what she hoped was a cavalier way, patted said chest and took a few steps back. "When was the last time you went for a run in the Fens?"

"Oh, man," he said, pushing a hand through his neatly trimmed brown hair. "I can't even remember."

Perfect. "How about you get settled here while I go to

the lab for a couple of hours? Then we can go for a run. Or walk. Whatever."

He laughed. Shook his head. "For your information, Miss O'Connel, I'm in excellent shape, which I know you know. You want to run? I'm in. But after that? We eat."

She didn't want to discuss dinner. A run was already on her schedule. For her it was a must, no matter how much work piled up. So it was the perfect solution. They could talk and get caught up with each other. Best of all, she'd be less likely to do something humiliating if they were doing something so casual. "Can you do ten miles?"

"I can, but I don't want to. I'd rather save time for dinner, even if it's just a quickie." He paused while she blushed three shades of red and then he continued as if he hadn't noticed. "If I remember correctly, a lot of unsavory folks hang out at the Fens."

"It's different now. It'll be nice. I go there a lot. Let's meet at Westland Gate."

Matt nodded, then said something she didn't catch. He'd shifted so that the sunlight coming in through the window picked up some gold in his brown hair. The past ten years showed in his handsome face. Fine lines fanned out from the corners of his eyes. His mouth was the same, only now there were long grooves bracketing each side, making him look a little more rugged and very sexy.

"Sam? Did you hear me?"

"Hmm?"

"I asked what time."

"Time for what?" She remembered as soon as he smiled. And dammit, her cheeks got hot. For the millionth time. Jesus. That makeup idea was sounding better and better.

IT TOOK HIM no time to unpack. He'd learned all the tricks. Had to, with all the traveling he did for work. But this was different. He hadn't taken any real time off in so long that he'd forgotten about relaxation brain. It was as if he'd taken a mild anesthetic, so everything was a bit hazy. A strong cup of coffee and a brief nap would solve that. Or a shower.

Coffee first, call his office second, his father third, then shower.

The coffee, it turned out, was simple to make and fantastic. He texted a note to his assistant about the brand, which he'd never heard of, determined to have it stocked in his New York office. There was an extravagant number of treats in the pantry—those gingersnaps turned out to be just the tip of the iceberg. His personal favorite, shortbread, was there—three different types of it. He liked them all. But he had to ration things like that because he still hoped to have dinner with Sam after the run.

He was on the phone for a few minutes with his assistant, Andrew, who'd been busy supervising the work they'd done in Budapest, where Wilkinson was buying land for a new hotel. Nothing new had come up, and they arranged to speak again in a few days.

Matt refilled his coffee before he speed-dialed his father's private line from his cell phone.

"Matt, I was just thinking about you," his dad said when he picked up. His old man wasn't that old. Sixty-two, and he worked out five days a week. Didn't smoke. Drank in moderation. Was still married to Matt's mother after almost forty years. "When are you coming to Boston?"

"I don't know. I'm taking some downtime before all the hoopla starts."

"Good for you. I told you about that new resort up-state, right?"

"Yeah, you did. It sounds great, but mostly I just want to sleep. You know how it is coming back from Asia."

"The work you did on the Tokyo job was top-notch. I've sent a report to the board. It'll help."

"Thanks. But we still have to get Bannister, Truit and Lee over to our side. Or at least one of them."

"It'll happen." His father sounded so sure. "Let me know when you're coming in. Will you be staying in the hotel?"

"I don't know yet. I'll give you a call."

His father made a sound, which was his way of saying goodbye, and Matt hung up the phone. Matt didn't make it a habit to lie to his father. He just didn't want to face work yet. The fund-raising gala was coming up, then the board meeting two days later, which would determine his future. Jesus, he hated that his life was out of his direct control.

For now, though, his most pressing concern was getting in the shower.

He pressed the remote that controlled the many, many jets in the shower proper, but he didn't explore their permutations, because he was too busy checking out all the creams and lotions. Sam hadn't skimped on anything. The body creams alone were worth several grand in total. La Mer, La Prairie, Guerlain. There were also sea-salt scrubs, high-end body washes and ridiculously expensive shaving gel. The Wilkinson Hotels were known for their luxurious accommodations, but even their finest suites didn't boast the cornucopia of indulgence that Sam had supplied. She'd even stocked his particular favorites.

Had to be pure coincidence since there was no way she could've known.

Her paying guests were never going to want to leave after staying here. He hoped she realized she'd be asked to customize the homes of private individuals. If he ever built a home, he was calling Sam first.

Thinking of Sam while his body was being massaged by water from neck to toe, he couldn't help imagining how much fun it would be to experiment on her. He'd use the La Mer, of course, and the Creed body wash. But that Acqua di Parma Magnolia Nobile shower gel was too sweet for him—perfect for her. Especially if he got to be the one to slather it on.

Oh, shit.

He wasn't allowed to masturbate to thoughts of Sam. Nohow, noway. He focused on other images. Like Sam in running— No. Even his tried-and-true go-to for nights when all he really wanted was to go to sleep wasn't cutting it. At last, after he turned the temperature on the jets way down, his libido calmed down, and he finished showering as quickly as he could.

By the time he got his towel, he was cold and angry that he didn't have better control over his thoughts. This was Sam. Jesus.

The only thing that might explain his traitorous brain was the contrast between the teenage Sam he'd known and the Sam he'd met today.

Regardless, he had to get a grip on his impulses. He shaved at the sink and tried out the Armani aftershave. After putting on his running gear, he had time to search Yelp for takeout by the Fens, in case she didn't want to come back to the apartment. They could just eat at Bravo if they finished running by seven thirty, but that didn't sound likely. Or they could grab a pizza or some burgers at one of the nearby take-out joints. Whatever was the quickest. He didn't want her forced to work half the night in order to squeeze in a meal with him. But it was just so damn good to see her that he'd selfishly snatch whatever time she'd make for him.

A quick look at his watch told him he had a half hour to kill before he left. So he called and ordered a taxi, then watched her awesome smart TV, where some nice person had left a recorded Manchester United game from earlier in the year. Another thing his travels had addicted him to: football. The soccer kind.

When his phone alarm went off, he flicked off the TV with a voice command, checked his wallet and key, got a bottle of water from the store that was Sam's kitchen, and went outside to wait for his cab. His heart was beating a little too quickly for a man his age. He should probably look into that.

4

ON THE BEAUTIFUL autumn evening, the Fens had a completely different vibe than the last time he'd been there. Plenty of runners were already in motion. Matt had arrived right on time, but Sam wasn't there yet. At least, not that he could spot. The thought of her made him smile. He remembered the feel of her hand on his chest, his arm around her trim waist. He'd been about to kiss her, but her soft gasp and shocked look had snapped him out of it.

His own shock had come later. He'd almost kissed Sam. Sammy. What the hell? He was her friend. Not even her close friend after all these years.

Didn't matter. He couldn't keep thinking of her as anything but a pal. He'd have to be careful, though. Reading the moods and needs of the girl had been relatively simple, but reading the woman? The thing was, he believed a lot of that girl was still in her. Far more than his college-age self was in him.

Marriage had helped change that, along with his career. Being the heir apparent made everyone think he didn't have to work hard, when it was just the opposite.

The last thing he wanted was to get into a leadership role via nepotism. The idea was abhorrent.

The London job would go a long way toward his proving his worth, assuming he made a success of it. He would.

He would.

The UK office had been sliding for over a year, and while Fairchild, the current manager, had been given a second chance, he hadn't brought it up to expectations.

Matt had been thinking about the changes he would've made for a while now. Not because he'd hoped the guy would fail. Matt simply had a clear vision of how he'd use the office to tap into the Scandinavian markets where Wilkinson Holdings had yet to find a stronghold.

He wondered if he'd ever convince Sam to visit London. It was one of his favorite cities and he could show her so many things. And if she'd come for a stay, he'd take her to Scotland and Ireland, too. It would be terrific.

That was if she'd leave her work for even a week. Which he couldn't see her doing. She seemed conjoined to her computer. Any real time away and she got antsy, just like back in school. Logan had mentioned he'd hardly seen Sam during his stay in Boston. Hell, Matt didn't even have the job yet, so there was no use thinking that far ahead.

Where was she, anyway? She was the one who'd set the time and place. Then again, the only time Sam cared about being punctual was when it was work related, and sometimes not even then. She'd once missed a deadline on her final paper in computer science, but after she turned it in, it had been so great the professor had given her an A regardless. When it concerned someone like Sam, rules became obstacles, and obstacles could be breached. He'd used that philosophy many times since his studies at MIT and Harvard.

Not that he could be much of a rule breaker. He was a Wilkinson, after all. He had a responsibility to uphold the family name. A shrink would probably tell him that was the reason for the reckless hobby he'd picked up back in school. His parents would've both had heart attacks had they known about the illegal street/mixed-martial-arts fights Matt had become involved in. Logan had been the one who'd figured out that Matt hadn't got buff by being on the rowing team.

Matt shook his head. Logan hadn't exactly been the voice of reason back then, and even he'd thought Matt had lost his mind. Matt did a bit of jumping and a few stretches while he kept an eye on the crowd, the street, hell, the sky, in case she dropped in by helicopter.

Finally, seven minutes after their meet-up time, Sam arrived, breathless and wearing shorts. Tight Lycra shorts that hugged her hips and butt, made extra visible by the short snug top she wore. He tried to look up from that inch of pale flesh that peeked out between her clothes, but it took a minute. "It's about time," he said.

"I'm sorry, but it's your fault."

"Mine?"

"Come on—let's start," she said, leading him onto the running path. Starting at a jog, warming up. He ran beside her for the most part. Except when someone else wanted to share the path, and he had to do the gentlemanly thing and fall back behind Sam.

It was pure luck he didn't trip and fall flat on his face when he got a view of her from behind. She was every bit as gorgeous as from the front. God bless the weather. It usually didn't get cold until Halloween, which was still two weeks away.

Once the path was clear again, he moved up beside her. "So why was it my fault you were late?"

"I had to rearrange my schedule for the next month."

"What? For a run?"

"Not exactly, but because I'm going to be late with the current project—which is really cool nano work, by the way—it set off a chain reaction. Let me tell you, Clark was not happy."

"I imagine he wasn't. But thank you."

"Why?"

"I'm hoping this new schedule will allow you to spend more time with me."

"It might. A little. If I don't get stuck on a problem."

"Understood." Evidently, that was the signal she'd been waiting for to kick their speed up a notch. Maybe two. He was up for it, though. Maybe he could work out some of the tension her shorts had caused.

"It must be really different since you were here last."

"What?" He hadn't noticed much besides the woman next to him.

"The Fens. I mean, it's all cleaned up. The track. They have so many activities on the green. I come here almost daily, either early morning or at dusk, like now."

He spared a glance at the park. It was pretty awesome. The waning twilight was turning the leaves into jewels, the grass a solemn green, and the pond, the part he could see, was crystalline.

"I actually have a recorder to take down any ideas that pop up while I'm running," Sam said, snagging his attention again. "And they usually do. It's supersmall and hidable and very good at focusing on the speaker and not the atmospheric noises."

"You're carrying a recorder?"

"It's under my top. I'll show you."

"Um…the recorder?"

She blinked at him. "Of course the recorder. What did you think?"

Matt smiled. "Are you recording now?"

They parted for a moment to let a small woman with two Irish wolfhounds pass. It was quite a sight. They were nearly bigger than their owner.

The moment he and Sam were back in sync, he looked at her confused expression. "I don't know, Sammy. You're really good at keeping my ego in check. It's the first time in years we're together and you can't just be present here and now?"

Her shock came as something of a surprise.

"No, wait. It's fine. I get it. I work a lot, too, and downtime is more of an idea than a practice. I sprang myself on you, and I'm sorry I caused you to change your schedule." He lightly bumped her elbow. "Tell you what. How about we at least grab a drink before I have to leave?"

Her pace slowed, and she was looking down instead of at the path ahead.

"I wasn't trying to make you feel guilty," he said. "I honestly understand what it's like to be buried in work."

He hoped she believed him. Not spending time with her would be a disappointment, more than he'd imagined before he'd seen her again. But now, when he realized the attraction thing wasn't going away, he needed to be careful. Her legs in those shorts? Her hair in a goddamn ponytail? Jesus. Yes, he'd do them both a favor by backing off.

She still hadn't said anything, which was worrisome, but he recalled that back in school she'd get quiet like this when she was trying to absorb new information or solve a problem. It gave him time to notice that almost every guy they passed was staring at her.

After an uncomfortable few minutes he saw they were checking her out both coming and going. One asshole was being a particular jerk and Matt gave him a warning look. The guy ignored him.

Matt shook his head with a wry grin. "You're going to get me in trouble again, aren't you," he muttered under his breath.

"What? What are you talking about?"

He hadn't meant for her to hear. "Uh, the guys who are ogling you as if they've never seen a woman before?"

"What guys?"

"All of them?"

A short bark of laughter sent her head back and her ponytail swinging. "You're imagining things. If anything, they're probably staring at you. And what did you mean by getting you in trouble again?"

"You know, that time I got the shiner. Back in the day?"

"I remember, but that had nothing to do with me."

"Are you joking? Of course it did."

"I wasn't even there. You were at a soccer game and some fans got rowdy. You also had a split lip and a good-size bruise on your chin. I think Logan got hurt, too. Rick was the only smart one and stayed out of it."

The hell he had. Matt snorted a laugh. Rick had jumped in neck deep right along with him and Logan. The bastard had just got lucky and come out of the fight without a scratch.

It dawned on Matt that they'd lied to her about that

night. A group of jocks had said some pretty nasty things about Sam, so the three of them had taken care of the problem, then made up the soccer story. Those guys had never bothered her again.

She'd got awfully quiet.

Matt looked over at her. She wasn't at his side.

He looked back. She hadn't just slowed down; she'd come to a dead stop in the middle of the path.

And she looked pissed. "Tell me what happened."

"It was nothing."

"Matt. Tell me. I can see it was no soccer game."

He walked back to her and pulled her to the side of the path so others could run through. "Look, none of us wanted you to know. That group, Kenny and his crowd, the jocks that used to come by? They said some stuff we didn't like. I admit I threw the first punch. But that was Logan's fault."

Sam's brows turned downward and she started walking toward the exit. He just had room to be at her side.

"What did Logan do?" she asked.

"He told me to stand back so I wouldn't get my 'pretty face' messed up. Of course I had to take the first shot. I got the shiner when I turned to flip Logan off and Kenny sucker punched me."

Sam stopped again and stared at him, her expression completely neutral. Until she burst out laughing.

"Why is that funny?"

"I didn't give a crap what those idiots said. I knew Kenny and his buddy Mark, and between them they couldn't come up with a grammatically correct sentence. How they got into MIT is anyone's guess."

She shook her head. Then her red-tinged eyebrows came together again. "Although I might have been hurt if they'd said really ugly things. I was pretty naive at the time. So thank you for defending my honor. And quite literally taking it on the chin."

He smiled, warmed by her thanks, her blush. The way the sun's last rays made her hair shiny like copper and her face golden. He couldn't help brushing a few strands of hair away from her eyes. "Anytime, Sammy." He nodded to the exit, just a few feet away. They'd clocked only about four miles, which meant they had some time. "So, what do you say about dinner?"

"Later," Sam said, not looking pleased. "Maybe."

"Come on, Sammy. We can get some takeout on the next street. We could eat it in a cab to your place, and then I'll take the cab back to the apartment."

"Eat in the back of a cab? No, thank you."

"Okay, we won't eat it until we're at your place."

She sighed and led him out into the bustle of downtown Boston, where she didn't stop until she hit the curb and raised her hand for a taxi.

"So," he said. "You leave me no choice. I'll have to call Clark to make sure you're getting the kind of nutrition that'll put a little meat on those bones."

She brought her hand down and faced him. "Matthew. When I was a kid, you and the other guys were the best thing I could have asked for. What you three did for my annoying self was beyond wonderful. And you're right. Back then I needed the nudge now and again. Okay, a lot. But I'm a grown woman now. I don't need you or Clark or anyone telling me when I should eat. If I'm hungry, I get food. Yes, sometimes I forget or skip a meal—everyone does. But I'm healthy, I assure you. I can take care of myself. No one needs to tell me what to do. Understand?"

She turned and threw her right hand into the air again, and a cab pulled up within seconds.

"Yes. I understand. I'm sorry. I hadn't meant any disrespect."

"I know that, you idiot." She went to the taxi door but didn't open it. Yet.

"Old habit—you got me there," he said. "That won't happen again."

"Thanks. But I really do have to work. I'll grab something on the way—"

"Yeah, but—"

"What did I just tell you about me being a grown woman?" She opened the passenger door. "Tomorrow. We'll have dinner tomorrow." Then she grabbed his shirt, pulled him down a few inches and kissed him square on the mouth. It wasn't a long kiss, and there was no tongue involved, but it shocked the shit out of him, and by the look on her face as she pulled back, her, too.

After clearing her throat, she darted into the taxi. But before the door slammed, she said, "Thank you for caring."

Matt put his hand on the edge of the passenger door. He stared at her for a few seconds. "Now you've done it, kiddo. I will find a way to know this new, beautiful grown-up woman. You can count on it." Then he stepped back to the curb and watched her taxi drive away until it became a blur among other yellow blurs.

"Well, I'll be damned," he said, then remembered he needed a ride home, too.

THE PICTURE ON Sam's computer showed a 3-D bridge being built by a Swedish company she followed on Facebook. Their printer was several levels above her new baby. The bridge had thrilled her when she'd first set eyes on it yesterday, and she'd immediately thought of seven different things she could build. She'd have to get a different kind of 3-D printer, but that was okay. When it came to work, she had no hesitation in buying the latest and best equipment. It was also the time she was most grateful about her success. Well, buying fancy printers could never compete with the day she'd bought a house in Cape Cod for her parents. That had been sweet, especially because she'd been able to keep it a secret until the paperwork went through. Talk about a great surprise.

Kind of like the surprise on Matt's face after she'd kissed him.

She'd kissed him.

Kissed Matt.

With her own lips. It wasn't anything epic. Not a *Titanic* kiss or a Mr. Darcy kiss, but *she'd* kissed *him*!

What the hell had she been thinking?

It wasn't even the kiss that was going to do her in, although she'd often thought that if she ever got the opportunity, she would literally die and go to heaven. But no. She was still here. Clark wasn't, which was good. All she needed was to have Clark come back for something or other he'd forgotten. Pity he didn't live farther away. When he caught her working late, he scolded her until she quit. Speaking of being scolded...

She'd said she was a grown-up. A woman to be reckoned with. That last part was implied. But it was all out there now.

A stand. That was what she'd taken. A STAND.

Which meant she had to start acting like a grown-up. Not just with Matt, either. She needed to dive into the

role with her whole heart. Until even Clark understood
he had no right to scold her for anything.

Oh, God.

It wasn't just taking the stand or kissing Matt on the
mouth that was going to cause havoc. She'd changed the
ground rules. She'd never—

The broken record of her thoughts jumped to another
track. The words he'd spoken at the end. Calling her
"kiddo"—that was pretty clever. But his challenge? How
could he possibly get to know the grown-up version of
herself unless she was that person?

Maybe she'd—

The door opened. Clark. Of course. He frowned at
her as he went to his desk. "Why are you wearing your
running gear?"

She looked down in surprise, but yes, he was right. "I
went running. I just got back a little while ago."

"Okay," he said, still glowering as if she'd stolen the
Arkenstone. "And didn't you say you were going to get
some sleep?"

"Well, yes, Clark, I did. And I will. I mean, why does
everyone want to tell me what to do? I'm fine. I'm great.
Fit as a fiddle. I'm not a waif begging for a meal. I said
I would get to sleep early and—"

"It's eleven forty."

Everything in her brain stopped with a screech. *Eleven
forty? Holy...* "P.m.?"

"Yes, p.m."

Sighing loudly, her head fell to her upraised hands.
When the internal lashing ended, she said, "Why are you
here so late?"

"I forgot my Deadpool comics for Jay."

She nodded a little. Boys and their toys. Who was she

to talk? She had the entire series of *Buffy* Dark Horse comics and far too many other collections. Graphic novels. Bobbleheads. Wonder Woman action figure. Lego sets from *Star Wars* and *Star Trek*. She moaned again and looked up, hoping Clark was gone, but no luck. He continued to scowl.

"You practicing for the Dour Looks Olympics? You can do better."

"I'm just reminding you of the things you asked me to."

"When I was a teenager. Maybe it's time to stop. It's been ten years, and you've been great at it, but maybe it's time I take responsibility for my life."

"Really?"

"Yes."

He thought about it for an achingly long time. But finally said, "Let's go a week. Then revisit."

She wanted to lay into him so bad, but she held back like an adult. Clark might have a point. She did miss a lot of meals when he was away. But that was then and this was Matt, so… "Fine. One week."

How hard could it be?

5

SAM BRUSHED A hand down her dress one last time before she walked into Row 34. That Matt had made a reservation for the same day was impressive, but then, the Wilkinson name was a powerful thing in Boston. She had arrived early, as she'd planned, which would give her time to rehearse so she'd be ready when Matt arrived.

The gleaming restaurant was already packed. She scoped out the crowd as she followed the host, her way illuminated by a long row of low-hanging lights. The industrial-chic seafood place hadn't changed much since the last time she'd been there, although the clientele seemed more upscale.

When she finally reached their table, Matt stood by his chair, smiling at her as if his early arrival hadn't ruined her chance to prepare. Damn. She clutched her purse, feeling the two stacks of three-by-five-inch cards she'd painstakingly filled with alternative versions of the speech she planned to make. Version A was simple. A nice but firm message that while it was lovely to see him, she had to put work first, so this would be their only dinner, but before he left Boston, they could meet for a drink. Period. Version B, on the other hand, wasn't simple at all.

She couldn't resist Matt's smile, and her heart couldn't help jumping with a mixture of excitement and want whenever she was in his presence. If she'd thought he was her dream man when she was sixteen, he was proving to be even more tempting to her at twenty-nine. God, he looked mouthwatering in his linen shirt tucked into worn jeans, with a sports jacket that pulled it all together perfectly. Matt had style coming out the wazoo and she was so glad she'd found her wrap dress still in the dry-cleaner bag.

She thanked the host and took her seat. Pointing to the brochure that sat in the middle of the table, she said, "You brought that?"

"I did," he said as he settled into his chair. "We'll talk about it later, if that's okay. First, you look beautiful. That's a great dress."

"Thanks," she said, willing herself to take the compliment and not tell him anything about the dry cleaner. "I got it for a security conference. I had to make a presentation."

"I bet you wowed them."

"It was cool because I was talking to techheads. They got it. When I had to talk to the CEOs…that was tricky. They all got glassy-eyed and kept checking their watches. Interestingly, almost all of them committed to buying stuff when they clearly didn't understand how it worked."

"Men are such idiots," Matt said.

Sam not only laughed but had an instant flashback to learning the art of dry humor from the man himself. Matt had been her gold standard, that by which she measured all humor. Except coding humor, which was always funny.

"It's so good to hear you laugh. Laughter is like fingerprints, I think. No two people do it exactly the same." He was quiet for a moment, took a sip of water, then met her gaze. "Although yours has matured," he said, his voice low and thoughtful. "Like a fine wine."

"Hmm," she sniffed. "According to Clark, my whining has become my defining trait."

Matt shook his head, his eyes on her the whole time. "I never remember you whining. The only thing you ever bitched about was gaming. Or comics. Never work. You loved solving problems."

So why couldn't she solve her Matt problem? Now that she was looking at him, it was doubly hard to execute plan A, which was also known as the Parachute Plan. The one that would eject her from the temptation and the turmoil, the nights of guilt-ridden masturbation.

At the mere thought, her cheeks felt hotter. She hid behind the menu, although she might have been too late. "Oh. They've changed the menu since I was here last. Did you see?"

"I've never been here. But— Never mind."

She uncovered her face. "No. No fair. Finish."

"Where's the waiter? I want some of that concierge beer."

"Tell me. I'll just annoy you until you do."

He laughed. "Good to know some things never change. Fine. I looked up the restaurant on Yelp. And TripAdvisor. And Facebook. And Chowhound."

She didn't want to laugh, but of course she did. "What did they say?"

"Eat here. Great oysters, great beer, great lobster roll."

"And with the addition of their incredible onion rings, you've just described what I'm going to order."

He smiled at her and covered her hand with his. She hadn't realized that she was leaning forward. Not boobs-on-the-table forward, but enough. He had really nice hands. They were big, with long, strong fingers and neat cuticles. His hands looked much better than hers. But keeping manicures took time. Besides, she rarely had reason to give much of a damn about her appearance.

Not that he seemed to care about her nails. The way he was looking at her, his dark eyes somehow darker even though the lighting wasn't that bright, plan B—where she had just enough sex with him to get him out of her system—was sounding better and better.

Their waiter, Xander, arrived. He called Matt "Mr. Wilkinson" and put bread and butter on the table before he told them the specials. In the end, the only difference between her order and Matt's was beer. He wanted the pilsner; she wanted the lager. Of far more importance was the fact that he'd moved his hand from hers, and she wanted it back. Now.

Which was not good. Not good at all. She'd have to go with plan A if she was going to survive his visit. At least she'd still have her imagination and her vibrator.

Taking in a nice deep breath, she quoted verbatim from her first three-by-five card. "It's been really good catching up with—"

"Hey, I forgot— Oh, sorry." He nodded at her. "Go ahead."

"That's okay. You go."

"We're building a new hotel in London. A big one, with over a thousand rooms. There's an existing hotel but we're stripping it down to the foundation and starting over. It's across the street from where they hold London Comic Con. I can't be any help next year, but the year after that, I can hook you up with a suite and food, even a limo pickup from the airport. Anything you want."

"You're kidding."

"Nope. I thought of you when we were putting the deal together. Have you been?"

"To the London con? Yes. Two years ago. I was on a panel for the game I helped design. It's all about lady dragons. Pretty awesome stuff. But yeah, it was fantastic. My only trip there and I didn't get to see much of the city at all."

"I think we should try to fix that. And also, you worked on a video game about lady dragons? That must have been—"

"A dream come true. It really was. It doesn't do all that well as a story, though, because it's pretty technical."

"And I'm one of those men in suits whose eyes glaze over?"

"I've always liked you better in jeans anyway," she said, grinning. "But seeing London sounds great." She sounded as cool as the water in her glass. But on the inside, there was absolute panic. What had he meant exactly? Had he just asked her to go visit London with him? But that wouldn't be for two years, when they could have sex right here in Boston, like, really soon…

She stopped. Just stopped the thought in its tracks. Having sex with Matt was not a good idea. She wanted him like crazy. He was a tall, gorgeous mix of the young man she'd had a crush on forever and a sophisticated dream she'd never forget. He was *too much*. It wasn't fair. No one could measure up to him, and then where would that leave her?

So. No more debate. She took a sobering sip of water, then repeated, "It's been really good catching up with—"

The beer arrived with much fanfare, because there was a real live Wilkinson in the restaurant. The concierge who delivered the brews went a little overboard in his descriptions of each one. Although, to be fair, her lager was so good it made her toes curl.

Finally, after a lot of smiling, the nice gentleman left but was quickly replaced by Xander, carrying a huge tray. He brought the fresh-caught oysters, lobster roll and onion rings they'd ordered but also a bunch of other sample plates. The tuna tartare was amazing, as was the crispy fish taco.

"I don't know how I'm going to be able to eat all this," she said, turning her attention back to her favorite dish, the oysters topped with a spicy cocktail sauce and lemon.

"No one is going to get upset if you don't taste everything."

"I want to. Are you kidding? And I'll be damned if I don't eat every last fresh oyster on this table. So beware."

"You honestly think you could take even one of my oysters?"

The dare was in place, just like in the old days. When she would have done exactly that. But she was an adult now. "It's been really good," she began, having to fight to keep it upbeat when it was now officially breaking her heart, "catching up with you—"

His cell phone rang. He sent her an apologetic look but took the call. Instead of scarfing down all the oysters while he was busy and not paying attention, Sam sneaked her cue cards out onto her lap.

She made herself read the first version of the speech.

The one where she was firm but nice. And wouldn't back down.

Then she pulled out the first card of the second version, but the tone of Matt's voice distracted her completely. He sounded so strong. So authoritative. She'd never actually heard him in business mode, and, whoa, he was clearly taking no bullshit from whomever it was he was speaking with. Someone who wanted to change a deal after they'd already signed papers, evidently.

He was quiet a moment, listening, then told someone named Andrew, in a very different and more Matt-like manner, that he'd be in the office in the morning to set up the conference call for 5:00 a.m.

He ended the call and frowned.

"If you have to go, we can get doggie bags or something."

"No need. I'm used to doing business at weird hours. Tokyo this time. We just finished up there, and now Takagi wants to mess with the non-compete clause."

"Sounds important."

"It's a pain in my ass. I haven't had a real vacation in years. Not since I was married. And that last vacation was what pushed us both over the edge. As soon as we arrived back in New York, Vanessa got the ball rolling on the divorce."

"That's... I'm really sorry it didn't work out."

"We married for the wrong reasons. No one's fault. The split was amicable. We see each other from time to time. Mostly in New York, but in Boston, too."

"Isn't that awkward?"

"Hasn't been. Anyway, this feels like a vacation, although I wish we had more time together." He held up a hand. "Not that I'm going to try and pressure you into taking more time off for me. Unless my sad story compels you in some way to—"

She laughed. It was so, so hard not to say yes. So she struggled for something else to say, something to do with his work, and came up with "I can't believe you have to make a conference call so early in the morning. You're the CEO's son. Don't they cut you any slack?"

Matt's smile changed, and she wanted to pull back the words.

"Hey. I was only teasing. You're not where you are because of nepotism. I know how hard you worked in school. I can only imagine what it took to get the *Harvard Law Review* your second year."

He seemed to relax, but she wished she knew him well enough to read what was behind the way he was looking at her. "You know about that, huh?"

"You're not the only one who reads the alumni newsletter."

The concierge arrived with a second round of beer, and she wished he hadn't. But maybe another drink would help her get up her courage. She had to tell him. Matt would understand. It was in both their best interests to cool things down. And it wasn't as if she wouldn't see him again. They'd meet for a drink one more time before he left. Simple.

MATT TOOK A big swig of his fresh beer and regretted it instantly. He had to get up at three thirty to prepare for tomorrow's call. He should have known Takagi was going to be a hell-raiser. He was the CEO's son, trying to make a name for himself. Matt understood where he was coming from.

Takagi would be tricky, but then, Matt liked tricky.

Nowadays, he used skillful legal maneuvering to outwit his opponents. In some ways it was similar to stepping into the ring. Or facing a rival in an illegal street fight. Only without the blood and bruises. He didn't need those badges of courage anymore.

"You're still upset, aren't you?" Sam said, watching him over the rim of her beer. "I swear I didn't mean anything."

"No. I know you didn't. Although, it's funny. My ex was stunned that I actually worked for a living. She thought, with my trust fund kicking in at thirty-five, I could take her on year-round yachting cruises or something. If anything, I've had to prove myself more than any other employee."

"What about your sister? Is she working for the firm?"

"Nope. She shops for a living, mostly with our mom. Which is where Vanessa got the idea that it was a family trait."

"I'm sure once she realized—"

"She didn't. I should have known after the first year that we were a mistake. She married the image of a Wilkinson and I married who I thought was everything I wanted. But I didn't know her, either."

Sam looked upset, which wasn't what he'd expected. His marriage was long over. He wouldn't make the same mistake again.

"Not to hijack the conversation," she said, "but wasn't Takagi the name of the boss at the Christmas party in *Die Hard*?"

His laugh got caught on a sip of water, and he coughed, nearly spraying the table. He shook his head. "You are such a weirdo."

She was already grinning, but that set her laughing. Talk about memories. They'd both called each other that so many times he couldn't count them all. Watching her eyes sparkle and her face glow pink from laughing, he wanted to end the dinner right then. Bribe or threaten her into going to the apartment with him, whatever it took.

But their waiter returned, this time, thank God, without more food or drink. He stooped down next to Sam and picked up what looked like a three-by-five index card, the kind she'd relied on back at MIT to keep her on track when she had a face-to-face with someone. "I believe this belongs to you." Sam's reaction was so outsize it stunned Matt. Her eyes got huge, her cheeks turned as red as cherry tomatoes and she ripped the card out of Xander's hand, causing a flurry of cards to spill all over the floor in front of her.

She made a sound of absolute horror as she dropped to her knees, first telling their waiter she didn't need help, then nearly shouting at Matt to let her get them. But it was too late. He saw just enough to know the cards were about him. And sex. Probably why it would be a bad idea for them to sleep together.

He handed her the card in his hand and helped her to her feet. She sat with her things a jumble on her lap. While he waited for her to get straightened out and the rest of the establishment to stop staring at them, he thought about his next move.

"Do I get to weigh in on the subject?" he asked. "Because I have a very strong opinion."

She turned even redder, which he could only tell because her gorgeous hair was pushed behind her suddenly pink ears. Finally, she stood so abruptly that if the chair hadn't been sturdy it would have tipped over. "I have to go."

"Sam," he said as she started to walk.

She stopped. Her back was to him, her body rigid with embarrassment. "Please," he said, his voice a lot quieter. "Come on. Sit down. I promise not to tease you, but we should really talk. We're both grown-ups, after all."

She turned mostly to glare at him, but then her shoulders relaxed a little. "Fine. But you can never use the grown-up card again. Are we clear?"

"As crystal."

She took her seat as he focused on not grinning. "So?" she said, sounding quite pissed. "Talk."

Matt lost any desire to grin or tease. He wanted this too much. "Look," he said, keeping his voice low. Private. "We're both buried in work. You right now more than me, but tomorrow morning the wheels will start turning, and who knows how slammed I'll be. But I know one thing for sure. If I can get some really good time off—I mean not looking at my calendar, not fielding phone calls, just relaxing—I'll do a better job when I go back to the grind. If that time is spent with you, it would be outstanding.

"I know you can't just take off work, but how about we both keep our evenings free for each other? I won't swear I can do it for a week, but for the next four days... That I can manage."

Her gaze moved from him to her purse, where she'd shoved her cue cards. He wished he knew what she was thinking. He knew what he wanted, but he wasn't going to press her. It had to be something she wanted, too. *Relaxing* could mean a lot of different things. A great many of them ending with orgasms.

He glanced at the brochure he'd brought along. Now, more than ever, he wanted a yes. He'd take three evenings. Two.

She sighed so long he had to stop himself from grabbing her hands and telling her to rethink her position. "Okay," she said.

He leaned back. "I didn't see that coming," he admitted.

"Me neither. But now that I've said it, I'm going to stick to it. To the best of my ability."

"Of course," he said. "That's only fair."

"Yes. Fair. Besides, we both have to eat, right? So evenings make sense."

He held back a telling smile. "Right. Eating." As if that were all she had in mind.

Sam stabbed the last bit of lobster on her plate. "Shut up, you weirdo."

6

MATT TOOK OFF his suit jacket, relieved that it was still early enough in the morning that no employees had shown up at headquarters yet. At a quarter to seven they'd start swarming off the elevators. What he needed to decide was whether or not he wanted his father to know he was already here in Boston.

He thought about loosening his tie, reconsidered and glanced down at his jeans. He'd sat at the conference table for the entire Skyped call, so he hadn't bothered with a full suit. But if he stuck around, he'd meet with more than a few raised eyebrows at this bastion of conservative values that was Wilkinson Holdings. There was nothing wrong with that in itself, but the company could do with some fresher voices. The firm was massive and hugely successful just the way it was and could weather storms that would flatten lesser conglomerates. It had strong footholds in international real estate, constructions, pharmaceuticals, small aircraft and, of course, the Wilkinson Hotel chain.

Matt had worked in every division, starting the day after he'd received his diploma from law school. Actually, even before that. He'd interned summers starting in high school. It was in his blood, this behemoth. The tax structures, the patents, trademarks, public relations, IT. The list went on, and on days like today, the mantle felt heavy. Constricting.

Although that was most likely because he hadn't got enough sleep. It felt as though it had been years since he'd woken refreshed. There were too many late nights and not enough downtime. Last night he'd been preoccupied by Sam. He'd have given anything to have seen all her cue cards. But the one he saw was good enough for him. The elevator dinged and he cringed. Just when he'd decided to slip out before anyone saw him. Wait. He still had a shot. Jacket in hand, he walked in the opposite direction from the lobby and down the hallway to the executive elevator. As he pressed the down button, he jerked at the sound of his name being called.

By his father.

He made sure his face was neutral and turned around. Charles Wilkinson stood in front of the open door to his office, frowning at Matt's jeans.

"What are you doing here? I had no idea you were even in town yet."

"Right. I'm not here officially. I've barely recovered from the Asia trip. But Takagi's son was trying to weasel his way out of the non-compete clause. I took care of it. Conference call."

"I see," his father said, undoubtedly noticing that Matt had conveniently left out the part about what he was doing at the office in Boston when he was still supposed to be at home in New York. "Is the kid going to become a problem?"

"I doubt it. Junior wants to prove he's the toughest hombre in town, so he's showboating. They weren't thrilled that we're planning a total overhaul of what was their flagship hotel. But it's all bluster. The contract is sound. He'll get tired of being a nuisance soon enough."

"Good," Charles said. "We don't need any drama this close to the board meeting."

Matt nodded.

"Come have a cup of coffee before you disappear."

"Did you make it?"

His father cracked a very small smile. "Shannon put it together last night. All I had to do was press a button."

"Okay, then. One cup." Matt let the elevator slip through his fingers as he joined his father in the suite that overlooked the Charles River. A portrait of Matt's great-great-grandfather hung in the place of honor above the least comfortable couch in the world. The old man's bookshelves were heavy, the carpet thick, and no computer had ever touched his big oak desk. The best thing about the office was the view, but the sophisticated coffee machine was a close second.

Matt let his father pour for them both, and they took their seats opposite each other in the big leather guest chairs. "You're worried about the board meeting. You think the vote's going to be that close?"

His father frowned at his cup. "Bannister and Lee are still on the fence. They both have their own ideas about how the London office should be handled. Truit is never going to vote for you. If we can't swing one of them…"

Sighing, Matt took small solace in the great coffee. "You'd think I'd have proved myself by now."

"You know better, Matthew. It has nothing to do with merit. You've proved your worth many times over. This is far more about me than you."

"I don't think that's quite true," Matt said.

"Regardless, now's no time to take risks or play loose with this Tokyo deal. All it would take would be one misstep."

"Right. One can be forgiven, but two?"

"Truit has the memory of an elephant. He wants to be right about everything and he did warn you about purchasing a company as new as Featherstone in the 2009 economy."

"Yes, yes. He did. And I went after them anyway." Matt had been fresh out of law school and maybe a bit brash, but Jesus, it was time to let it go. "I'm ready for London, Dad. I mean it."

"I believe you. But the board will vote for whoever they think will make them more money."

"As long as it doesn't involve anything to do with the twenty-first century."

"It's not that bad. The plans for the hotel you're bickering about are ultramodern. You did well there, son. Your input on the deal was invaluable."

He could never say his father wasn't on his side. Which was a good thing. Despite his silver hair and the brutal hours he worked, he was as sharp as he ever had been. Though Matt sometimes wondered if his dad still worried he might make another rash decision.

"So, Takagi's son. He's gunning for…?"

"His father's approval, basically." Matt shrugged. "Legally, he doesn't have a leg to stand on."

"Is that why you seem so agitated?"

"No." Matt unclenched his jaw, annoyed that he'd let his unease show. "I didn't like him. He's not interested in making his own mark. He wants to displace someone.

As publicly as possible." All true, but that wasn't what was bothering Matt.

"Keep him controlled. Don't bring your ego to the table."

Matt finished his coffee and stood up, grabbing the jacket he'd slung over his leather chair. "I need to go before anyone else sees me. We'll speak before the gala."

"Are you bringing someone?"

"Doubt it," he said. He thought about the fund-raiser all the way down the thirty-nine floors to street level. Pity Sam wasn't into parties. He had a feeling she'd rather chew off her own arm than show up at a damn gala with more than five hundred guests.

But it didn't make him want to take her any less.

THE MOMENT MATT stepped outside the Wilkinson Holdings building, he called the folks who would be handling the surprise he'd planned for Sam tonight. Apparently they weren't in yet, and he probably didn't need to confirm, since he'd spoken to them last night, but he left a message anyway. It could all go south if the timing didn't work out.

Around him, crowds of people were rushing to work, and he had nothing to do all day but wait for Sam. Well, if he wanted to review some contracts, yeah, sure, there was plenty to do. But he was too restless and edgy. He needed to burn off some negative energy. Banish the thoughts of the one big mistake he'd made early in his career.

It wasn't as if he'd lost all that much money for the company. He'd bet every one of those guys sitting on the board had made more than one error in judgment in the time they'd been there. That the risk he'd taken was still held against him pissed him off. And the fact that his father felt it necessary to warn Matt about his behavior made him sad.

He'd had offers from other firms. Top-notch legal firms that would have paid him whatever he asked. But he would never know if they had just been buying his name, and that wasn't for sale. He wasn't for sale.

One of the reasons he wanted the London job so much was to prove, once and for all, that he wasn't a man easily defined, and certainly not by one misstep. That he had no control over whether he got the job or not was so damn frustrating...

He smiled, knowing exactly what he needed. And hailed a cab.

When he reached the ugly Southie warehouse, it wasn't even 8:00 a.m. yet. He wondered if he'd know anyone inside. Probably a few.

He walked in, and the first thing that hit him was the smell. The sweat that was like a fog had almost gagged him the first day he found the place. This was the stink all the upscale gyms did everything they could to abolish. Kind of disgusting, but at least his tolerance for it had held since college.

Then came the stares, though far fewer than all those years ago. Boxing as a body workout had gained favor with the millennials, and the ratio of hard-core boxers to those who would never dream of boxing as a profession had shifted. He was met by a couple of wolf whistles, however. He cursed himself for forgetting about his tie and jerked it loose.

At the back end of the building, the door to the office he was looking for was open and he heard the old man's rusty voice before he saw him. It occurred to Matt that his ex-trainer had probably forgotten him. Didn't matter.

"I'll be damned," Carrick Moynihan said, standing up behind his battered desk. "It's the fancy one come back."

Matt held out his hand. "You forgot my name? I'm hurt."

"Hell, I know who you are, Matty boy." Carrick grinned. The guy was still missing a front tooth, but his black Irish hair was now white. "You look good. What are you doing here?"

"You've hardly changed, Carrick. Still skinny as a snake and twice as charming. I'm looking to spar. I'd have to borrow a pair of gloves."

"You'd have to borrow a magic wand, too. When's the last time you were in a ring?"

"It's been a while."

Carrick moved around the desk and punched him in the gullet. It wasn't a hard punch, but Matt hadn't prepared for it. "What the hell?"

"You're in no shape to spar," Carrick said. "Why don't we just give you some gloves, let you work on a bag?"

"I work out with a bag. That's not why I'm here. You never used to be worried I'd get hurt."

"You were younger. You healed better."

"I was thinking how much I missed you, you old prick. I'm not looking to make this a regular thing, okay? It's not like back in college. I've got a lot of tension to work out, that's all. You got someone I can go against or not?"

The older man—he must have been sixty at least—shook his head. "Your funeral."

That itch in his chest started to feel better as soon as his hands were taped and he got a good look at his sparring partner. The guy was around Matt's age. Fit. Hopefully, they would be evenly matched.

The idea wasn't quite as shiny when he stepped into the ring. He'd had the time and he should've gone by the apartment to change first. He'd hung his dress shirt and was down to a white T and his jeans, which wasn't ideal, but doable. But he wore the wrong shoes. They wouldn't keep him near as steady as he needed to be. Sure, he worked out with a bag, but the bag didn't hit back.

This was one of the stupidest ideas he'd had in a long time. He hadn't been so foolish as to decline the protective headgear, but it was no guarantee he wouldn't get marked. The gala was coming up. If he walked in with a shiner or a swollen jaw, it would spook the board members and he'd kiss the London job goodbye.

But instead of doing the smart thing, leaving, he leaned in at the handshake and said, "Do me a favor, huh? Don't mess up my face."

The guy started laughing and then announced the request to his trainer and the rest of the room, but he agreed.

All Matt could do was let the laughter slide off his back. He was in great shape. He could do this.

It felt damn good to land two straight rights in a row.

Less so when his opponent abandoned the jabs and the pitty-pat punches and nailed him with a right hook to the ribs.

As the sun inched slowly down, Sam stood in front of the apartment door, knowing Matt probably knew she was there. She hesitated anyway. She was hungry, which was good, because no matter which chef's brochure he'd chosen, the food would be excellent. She'd purposely worn comfortable clothes, not wanting to send any kind of message, especially because they weren't going out. Her black jeans were old favorites and who knew how the pink bowling shirt had come into her possession, but she liked it. Since the warm weather from last evening had taken a turn for the bitter, she'd pulled on her camel coat. She carried her big black tote bag as a purse.

It was the tote that had her worried. She'd put her overnight kit inside. Panties, a T-shirt, socks, toiletries, condoms, a little makeup, a brush. Everything that shouted one-night stand so loudly she was positive Matt would take one look at her and know she'd decided to go for plan B.

In her defense, she'd made her final decision for the good of her work. Not that she'd tell Matt that. Her brain was too full of wanting him, and she wasn't concentrating properly. Clark had noticed, of course. And even though she hadn't said what was bothering her, he probably knew.

Right now, though, work wasn't her main concern. So many things could go wrong. The most important of which was she might lose Matt's friendship.

No, even if Matt did figure out she'd brought condoms in her purse, it didn't mean she couldn't change her mind. He would never press her for more than she was willing to give.

She rang the doorbell, grinning at the sound of the MP3 playing the first twenty seconds of "Immigrant Song." At least she didn't have to worry about Matt finding out suddenly that she was a weirdo. He'd known that from the get-go.

The door swung open, and his smile hit her right in the flutters. It made breathing a little difficult.

"You have a key," he said with that dry voice that always made her smile.

"I'm not going to barge in on my guests. I wasn't raised by wolves."

"No, maybe robots. Or cyborgs. Probably cyborgs. Come on in."

She stepped into the room, and Matt was suddenly coming at her, his face close enough that she didn't even think—she just turned so his lips would touch hers.

She could feel him jerk a little, and that was when she realized he'd been going for a cheek kiss.

Swell.

But the man was quick. Before she could even lean back, he'd pressed in, changing the cool lip-on-lip stalemate into what felt like a real kiss. No tongue, though. She put her mixed feelings aside about that, mostly because she'd seen something, people, probably the servers or the chef, standing in the space between the living room and the kitchen.

Matt let her pull back, and his eyes met hers square on as she did. He grinned again. "Hey. You're here."

"I am," she said. "It smells like honey and strawberries. Are we having dessert first?"

"Uh…no. In fact, I'll take your coat. You can take the rest of your clothes off in the second bedroom. The robe is already laid out on the bed."

"Excuse… What?"

"Coat? Purse?"

Sam leaned to her right until she could see past Matt. The two people, one male, one female, were dressed in white as chefs would be, but they weren't there to prepare food. There in the living room were two massage tables set up side by side. Something soft played over the apartment speakers, and the smell inside changed from supersweet to sweet with a spicy edge.

She stood up straight again. "Massages?"

He nodded. "Couples massage. We did agree to try out some of the recommendations from the brochure."

"But I thought you were bringing a chef in."

"If you're hungry after, we can find something to eat."

One more peek past her wily friend proved the massage setup was real, not a hallucination. At least, she didn't think so. She reached over and pinched Matt's arm, just in case.

"Ow. What did you do that for?"

"Checking."

"You're supposed to pinch yourself, you nutcase. Now, come on. I think we can both use ninety minutes of pure bliss."

"That long?"

"What, you don't like—"

"No, no. I do. I just don't get them often because I'm usually preoccupied with other stuff."

"Everything's ready," he said, standing back and sweeping his arm in front of him like a game-show host.

"You're not naked."

He nodded. "Keenly observed. But I didn't want to freak you out when I opened the door."

"Too late."

"Go," he said. "Just leave your stuff in the other room. Come back when you're ready. Don't worry. This is Kathy and Duncan and I explained to them that we're friends, so they'll make sure I don't flash you and vice versa, okay?"

That made her relax a bit. Then she remembered what was in her purse. Maybe she should tell them to go ahead. Flash away.

Nope. There was no way that was going to happen. She wasn't fond of undressing in front of other people. Not even doctors. Or men she'd slept with. She was a lights-off kind of gal, and this seemed very…bright.

Matt cleared his throat. It got her moving. She tried not to look as if she was running as she hurried to the bedroom. It took a few minutes to get up the nerve to take off her coat.

She was going to hear Matt's sex noises during the massage. No doubt about it.

And he'd probably hear hers.

It shouldn't have been an issue, now that she'd decided to sleep with him, but…

She sat down on the edge of the bed and took a few deep breaths. Maybe this was the best plan ever. Instead of going from dinner straight to sex, there was now this little trial period. One where she'd get to hear his noises. Picture him naked under the sheet. Hell, if she hated it, she could always leave. Standing up, she started to take off her various layers. Toed off her shoes and was tempted to keep her socks on, but no. She stripped. Undressed. Got naked. Bared her butt.

She was in her robe faster than she could say her five favorite swearwords.

Oh, God. This was going to be terrible. Or wonderful. She'd dreamed of naked Matt a lot in her life. But in her dreams, she was sexy, too. Not the skinny, geeky girl who didn't get out much.

She closed her eyes, counted to ten, put on her bravest face and walked out to meet her destiny.

7

MATT TOOK A deep breath when Sam walked into view. He'd already figured out what to do if she declined his invitation. As he had taken the precaution of paying the massage therapists ahead of time, they were fine with wrapping things up at his signal. Thankfully, Sam had got undressed. Although she could have easily been wearing her underwear underneath that thick robe.

He didn't care. Sam in her underwear would still be sexy as hell. Though he'd have felt a lot better if she hadn't looked as if she were headed to the gallows. "Kathy and Duncan brought an excellent bottle of champagne with them," he said. "Would you like a glass?"

She hadn't quite met them halfway. Her gaze kept skipping from him to the massage therapists, then to the portable tables and the accompanying assortment of oils and wrapped items.

He'd dimmed the lights, the walls had turned pale blue and the fireplace crackled. Soft music and exotically scented candles completed the atmosphere. "If this were a real couples-massage night instead of a demo," he continued, taking a few steps toward Sam, "we would have had a soak in that big tub in the master bath first."

"That's right," Kathy said. "We usually begin each massage with a relaxation soak." As she went on to describe the possibilities that came with a couples massage, Matt kept his eyes on Sam. Not just because he was hoping to see what was under that Turkish robe. He was watching her for signs of skittishness.

Her eyes widened, but it wasn't fear that he saw.

When Kathy wound up the very long list of available options, Sam said, "That sounds… How long would that take?"

Matt grinned. "Hey, if you want to try them all, I'm game."

"No, I meant if I wanted to try that tech-massage thing and the deep tissue, how long would that take?"

"Ninety minutes," Kathy said. "Approximately."

Sam looked at him. "Do you have a lot of spa days under your belt?"

"A few. I know I'm going for the deep tissue myself. What do you say? Willing to give it a shot?"

Her smile came slowly. "Sure. Why not?" She was almost convincing. "I'll have that champagne now," she said before she turned to Kathy. "I'd like what he's having and the tech, please."

"Absolutely. Would you like me to work on you, or would you feel more relaxed with Duncan?"

She looked down at her bare feet. "You'll be great," she said. "No offense, Duncan."

The big guy nodded. "None taken."

Matt brought her a flute of Perrier-Jouët, along with one for himself. "You don't have to do this, you know."

"I want to," she said with an upward lilt on the last word.

"Then here's to new adventures," he said, clicking his glass against hers. They both drank the champagne more quickly than it deserved. When she handed him her empty flute, her gaze slipped down his robe and she wet her bottom lip. This was either the best idea he'd ever had or the worst.

THERE WAS NO way there wouldn't be sex.

Sam knew without a doubt that once she took off her robe and slid under the sheet, the night would end with her and Matt in bed together. Something she'd never thought would happen, but there it was, complete with champagne.

Which, she had to admit, was giving her courage. The massage might also help relax her—at least, she hoped it would, because she didn't want to be awkward when it came to… Oh, who was she kidding? Awkward was in her DNA.

Kathy held up a sheet while Sam dropped her robe and climbed up onto the table. She was a little disappointed that it wasn't equipped with a face hole, but then she looked left and understood why not. Matt was right there, dropping his robe behind a sheet. When he lay down, their eyes met. Of course. The whole thing was about connection.

Not only were they looking at each other, but they were both naked.

She immediately tensed. Kathy's warm, velvety hands touched her back, and she focused on her breathing: inhale for seven counts, hold for four, exhale for eight. The rhythm of her breathing sent her quickly into an alpha state, where she was halfway between fully awake and completely asleep.

Everything smelled heavenly, Kathy knew what she was doing, and it was as if Sam had been transported to an alternate reality where she got to look deep into the eyes of the man she'd had a crush on for all these years.

Of course, every time it occurred to her that she was blatantly staring at Matt, she had to look away. But she couldn't look away for long. After the fifth or sixth time, he grinned, and she grinned back, and then she let herself stare unabashedly.

Many long, languorous minutes later, Kathy whispered, "We're going to do some deep-tissue work now. If anything is uncomfortable, tell me and I'll adjust, all right?"

Sam thought about telling her to just keep on doing the soft massage, but she didn't want to seem like a wuss.

Two minutes later, Sam had to ask for a gentler rub. Kathy instantly obliged, and then things got interesting. Not with Kathy...

With Matt.

It looked as if Duncan was shoving his elbow halfway through Matt's back, but Matt didn't even wince. She knew because his suddenly intense gaze was locked on hers, the smile gone. It was as if he'd turned up the dimmer switch all the way. She didn't even want to blink.

Time slid by in a haze. She felt completely grounded in her body and apart from it at the same time. The two other massages she'd experienced hadn't been anything like this. But then, Matt hadn't been there, his gaze hungry, his lips slightly parted, and, God, she could see his nostrils flare. Who knew that would turn her on so much?

The lower-body work presented a completely different kind of challenge for Sam. It wasn't intrusive or anything like that, but her thighs weren't used to kneading hands.

Now her own lips parted as she started to pant. The heat seemed to rise by ten degrees and it was everything she could do to stay focused.

This was the weirdest foreplay ever.

It didn't help that the walls around the living room had changed from soothing blue tones to pulsing dark pinks. She'd thought about turning off the sensors and then had forgotten about it. But she was glad she'd left them on when she heard Kathy's sharp inhalation as the colors began undulating, and now, well, now Sam was experiencing the full effect of what a couples massage could do.

It took her a moment to realize Kathy was speaking to her. "Samantha, would you like to turn over now?"

She really didn't. What she wanted was to keep this barely controlled sizzle going. For Matt to sweep her into the bedroom, where they could do wonderfully wicked things to each other all night long.

"I think we're good," Matt said, clearly reading her mind.

Sam shivered down to her toes.

"We'll get your sheets back to you soon."

The therapists didn't even comment. They simply stepped away, their backs turned as Matt climbed off the table, covering himself with the white sheet. It didn't hide the tent pole down below.

She slipped off her table, the sheet a comfort because this was really happening. The best thing was that Sam hadn't lost her alpha-state buzz. She felt as if she were floating, more at ease than she'd have ever believed. They didn't touch on their way to his room, but that didn't mean they weren't on the same wavelength.

The moment Matt closed the door behind them, he pulled her into his arms.

HE'D WANTED TO kiss her since that first day she'd let him into the apartment. And at last, thank God, she was his. Their sheets tangled as he searched for bare skin. Once he touched her back, he smiled, still managing to kiss her with everything he had.

His eyes were closed but he could still map out her irises in his mind. They'd locked on to each other on the massage tables. Prolonged eye sex as foreplay was hotter than he'd ever imagined.

Sam was new to him. He'd never felt her body like this. Never tasted her as she tasted him right back. He moaned into her mouth and her breath hitched, which just made him want her closer, although there wasn't much closer to get.

He'd been hard for a hell of a long time. There was no hiding it. He didn't even want to. Except…

Pulling away wasn't any fun. "Are you sure you want this?" he asked.

Her eyes were dark, the pupils showing only a hint of green. "Yes." She blinked. "I understand completely, okay?"

Her response was a little odd, but when she pulled him down into another kiss, he forgot all about it.

As he teased her tongue and nibbled on her lush lower lip, he heard the ocean. Waves crashing on the shore. He'd have said that was impossible, but this was Sam…

The sheets had to go. He wanted to see her. To feel her, skin on skin. To discover her secrets and make it so good for her, for them, that they'd never forget it.

When he stepped back this time, he caught a glimpse of the far wall, and it stopped him. The ocean. Right there. On all the walls. Big waves, vivid as an IMAX picture, only private and theirs alone. "How?"

"What?"

He nodded to the left.

"Oh, it's perfect. I've only seen it by myself, but this is so much better."

"How did you do that?" He'd always thought of her as a techie, but his Sammy had quite the whimsical spirit.

She tugged the hair at his nape. "Really? You want to talk about that now?"

Laughing made it harder to kiss, so he let go of his chuckles along with his sheet. Thankfully, there wasn't too much bruising from his workout this morning, and Duncan had been careful to keep away from his lower chest.

Sam held on to her sheet, although it wasn't quite hiding everything. The glimpse of one areola against her pale skin made him groan.

She, on the other hand, was too busy staring at his erection to notice.

"Everything okay?"

"Recalibrating," she said. Finally, her gaze meandered up to his shoulders, his face, his eyes. "You're gorgeous. I never— I mean, I've seen you in shorts and without a shirt, but that was—"

"A long time ago. Another life. In this one, you're the gorgeous one. I'm just a lucky bastard."

She smiled, inhaled deeply and then dropped her sheet. "Fair's fair," she said, but her eyes slammed shut as her blush painted her from chest to cheek.

Everything he saw was beautiful.

There was no doubt she was a true redhead. That made his cock jerk, although so did looking at her shoulder. Rubbing her arm down to her hand, he said, "Come with me?"

"Okay." Her grip was strong as he led her the short distance to the bed. He pulled the blankets down to the floor. She lay down, put her head on a pillow, arms by her sides, legs tightly together, stiff as a board.

"I see the massage got you nice and relaxed."

She looked down at herself and burst out laughing. Then her gaze fell to his cock, which was practically touching his stomach. Her excited shiver and breathy exhalation were just the green light he needed.

WATCHING MATT CRAWL into bed next to her was surreal and sexy beyond words. She wasn't able to take her eyes off him. It reminded her of a dream. Of many dreams with him as the star, but they'd been—

His knee brushed her thigh, and okay, this was definitely not a dream. The waves continued to crash around them, the scent of the ocean mixing with the fragrant oils from their massages an aphrodisiac. The room changed colors as the CGI sunset filled the space with orange, pink, blue and yellow. His eyes flashed dark and hungry, and he startled her when he slid down the side of her body.

He stopped with his head just above her clamped thighs. He bent, nuzzled the small triangle of hair. His inhalation made his eyelids flutter. Then he touched the tip of her lips with the tip of his tongue.

At first she squeezed her legs even tighter together, but as soon as her body would allow it, she let go of her resistance. This was it, her one shot at an actual fantasy coming true. She'd meant it when she told him she understood. This might be their only time together and she didn't want to regret a single second of it. She whimpered at his first touch. Gripped the bottom sheet with both fists.

All he used was his tongue, licking her just enough to make her blush deepen and her heart race. It wasn't long until he started moving again, a panther crawling up the length of her.

He stopped again when his mouth was over her chest.

"Oh, God," she cried out. "What are you…? That's… Oh, God."

He didn't stop sucking her right nipple at her outburst, although he did chuckle. At first it was all she could do not to grab his head and hold it there.

His mouth was so wet, his tongue pointed as he flicked the sensitive tip of her nipple. His moan caused his lips to vibrate very subtly.

Keeping her eyes open wasn't easy in spite of the incredible show taking place all around her. The sunset colors painting the walls came in a distant second to the way he looked at her. This wasn't Dream Matt or Crush Matt. This was real. She wanted to memorize everything, every lick and every sound.

Matt started in on her left nipple but teased it for only a few seconds before he raised his head and hovered over her, his eyes level with hers. "You're so beautiful," he said, his voice gruff, as if he'd just woken up.

That was only testosterone and arousal talking, but she didn't mind.

"I mean it, Sammy." His eyes stayed locked on hers. "So how about you believe me?"

She inhaled and then let the air go. "All right," she said, looking away and up at the ceiling. "The sun's about to set on our indoor ocean, and I can see Venus up there. Anything's possible."

"I can't even guess how you've done this."

"Magic," she said. Just like now. The whole evening. It was all magic.

"How come I never saw this fanciful side to you?"

She almost said it was because he'd practically avoided her during his last two years at MIT.

But then he saved her from herself by kissing her nose, then her lips. He pulled back when she touched his cheek.

"What do you want, Sam? Whatever it is, I want you to have it."

Still touching his face, she looked at his chest, the dusting of dark hair, his toned muscles, his patient erection. "Would you be offended if I told you I don't want a lot of foreplay?"

He laughed and she felt his mouth shift in her palm. Touching him like this grounded her. Made her want more. She tugged him down and wrapped her legs around his waist.

"Offended? No. It's taken everything I have not to ravage you."

"Really?"

"God, yes. Feel my chest."

She rested her palm over his heart and felt the drumming within his chest and how he was trembling. "Oh," she said. "So I'm not the only one."

"No," he said, leaning down to steal a kiss. "The condoms are all the way in the bedside drawer."

"That's really close."

"Yes. But it means I have to move. Promise you'll remember exactly where we were when I get back?"

It was her turn to laugh. "I promise. Good grief, you'll be seconds."

"It's the flow, Sammy. Now, just hold that thought."

When he dislodged her legs, she understood what he meant about the flow. They'd been in a bubble just then, one that didn't concern itself with the practicalities of life.

Good thing he'd remembered the protection.

His hiss made her look. He'd rolled the rubber on, getting that out of the way, and before she could blink, he was back where he'd been, and her legs were hugging his waist.

He completed his kiss, making sure she understood exactly what was going to happen. Thrilled and anxious, she touched him more, running her hands over his broad back and sides. "I doubt I'll ever be more ready than this."

"Yeah?"

She nodded. "I want you inside me, Matthew."

"Oh, Christ," he murmured, more to the air than her. Seconds later he was balanced on one arm while his free hand guided his cock. His eyelids fluttered again, making his unfairly long lashes brush the tops of his cheeks. His lips parted on a moan as he entered her.

It didn't matter that she wanted to remember everything. It happened too quickly, her rush as well as his.

He thrust again, clenching his teeth together, as if trying to slow down, but the feral way he sounded, the flaring of his nostrils, the flush on his face, made her writhe beneath him with need.

After shifting for better traction, he entered her again. Harder. He pulled out more slowly, but it didn't take him long to repeat the powerful thrust.

She found herself keening, failing to trap the sounds of her pleasure behind closed lips.

"Let me hear you," he said, his voice so low it rumbled straight through her.

"I just…"

"What?"

"Just don't…"

He slowed, and she panicked, tugging on his hair. His head jerked back.

"Sorry. Sorry. Just don't stop."

He choked out a laugh. "Okay. But you'll have to let go of my hair."

She did just that, and he made her forget about her embarrassment when his next push moved them both up the bed.

"I want to—" His words trailed off in a groan as he found a new rhythm, one that drove the act to another level.

"Yes," she said, more breath than sound. It was the only word she could find. With every thrust her whole body shimmered with pleasure. It had started low in her belly but had spread like a low fire through her thighs and her chest. She felt the beginning of a climax pooling deep. "Oh, my God, Matt."

"Christ, Sam. I'm not going to last."

"Don't you dare stop."

A drop of his sweat hit the tip of her chin. "Sam," he said again, his voice raspy, his shoulders and arms straining. "Sam," he echoed, turning her name into a desperate plea.

Then, impossibly, he moved faster. So fast it was crazy sexy, and it made her reach down between them with her free hand to take herself the last few seconds to orgasm.

She cried out. Loudly. Right in his ear, but he didn't

seem to notice. His body stiffened, and he got that look on his face.

She didn't care. She was too busy riding out the aftershocks and trembling, memorizing the feelings so she could replay this again and again in her mind.

Eventually, his head drooped. He backed up in the nick of time, or he would have hit her chin with his forehead.

"Holy crap, Sam. That was over way too fast."

"No, it wasn't," she said, her voice almost back to normal. "It was perfect."

"Yeah, it was kind of perfect."

"Perfect," she whispered, no modifier needed.

"But next time, we'll take it slower."

Next time? She shivered. It wasn't just an aftershock, either. There was going to be a next time!

8

MATT HAD FINALLY cooled down and let the night roll on. It wasn't like him to go so hard and heavy so quickly. Usually, he'd have the condom under his pillow; he'd have brought water bottles for two. It wasn't as if he hadn't had time to get ready, but he had forgotten. He'd been too busy worrying about her reaction to the massages.

He pulled her close so he could feel her beautiful body against his. It made his cock twitch. Not that he could do much about it. Yet.

Sam shuddered.

"You cold?"

"A little."

He kissed her forehead, then rolled away to the side of the bed and sat up.

"Where are you going?"

"To pull the blankets up. Then I'm going to the fridge."

"Oh, there should be grapes. And cookies. And milk."

"Anything else?"

Her eyebrows went down as she thought about the question. "Make sure you bring the white chocolate chip macadamia cookies."

"I promise," he said, watching her smile contentedly. He was pretty satisfied himself. He'd hoped it would be good between them, but so far, it was off the charts.

After he put on his robe and made sure she was warm, he made his way to the kitchen. Luckily, he'd spied a decent lap tray in an earlier foray, so he got that out and piled on grapes, a bottle of milk, two glasses and, of course, cookies. His favorite, Walkers shortbread, and the ones she'd requested, plus some gingersnaps for the hell of it.

He almost whistled on the way back, which was nuts. He didn't whistle. But the walls told his story. They were blushing pink. Too girlie by far, although he had to admit, they were onto something. The massage had been outstanding, and his time with Sam?

"Epic," he said as he returned to the bedroom.

"What?"

"I bring a feast. And I forgot napkins." He put the tray down and headed out again.

"Wait."

He turned.

"I don't mind crumbs in the bed."

He grinned and joined her. Sam was sitting against the headboard, and he put the tray between them. "This is a really fancy-ass place. So don't be so devil-may-care about those crumbs."

"Devil-may-care?" Her grin was great. "I know the owner. She won't mind."

He laughed, while she dug in as if she hadn't eaten in days.

"Are you sure you don't want anything else? Like a chicken on a spit?"

"Be careful there, big guy. I like my cookies and milk."

"I can tell. You're making me want one of yours."

"Oh, no. After that chicken-on-a-spit comment?"

He smiled. It was so easy to do with Sam. Then he doled his portions out on the small amount of room she'd left him. It was fine. It was all great. Even laughing with his mouth full didn't bother him. Except that he really did have to go get some napkins.

WHEN MATT HAD mentioned the next time, she hadn't dreamed he meant forty minutes later. It had started after they'd wolfed down their cookie dinner. She'd snuggled up close to him, and he'd held her tight. It was soft and sweet. They reminisced in low voices for a while. Nothing that mattered. They spoke mostly with touches and smiles and little kisses that had grown into serious making out, and then he got hard and she trembled, knowing what was coming next.

This time, he did move slowly. He had each one of her legs over his shoulders, his fingers spreading her wide as his mouth did every wicked thing that could be done with a tongue.

Sam was barely holding it together. Since the sheets had been thrown off the bed again, she had to grasp the bottom sheet with both hands, or else she was afraid she'd pull his hair out.

She jerked as he sucked her clit into his mouth. It was a first, something no one had done before, and it was about to make her scream. Her body jerked again.

He released her, soothing her with long, tender licks. Moaning, he used his fingers inside her. But he didn't take her all the way.

Instead, just as the telltale shift deep and low within her told her a climax was on its way, he moved up so he could kiss her. Their gazes locked, and it was the second thing that had never happened to her before. She felt as if she was looking into his soul.

When he entered her, it was…more than perfect.

MATT HAD TO STOP. Just stop for a minute, look into her eyes again, get centered. Sam was his tonight. He hoped it wouldn't be only tonight. But there was no way to know for sure.

He wasn't about to complain. Maybe it was because they'd had this eye-contact thing going on that he felt so in sync with her. He wasn't sure what to make of it. He tended to avoid deep gazes fraught with meaning. Now that he was in her again, he couldn't help feeling as if their connection was far more than a simple gaze.

Sam was the first to close her eyes, to break the slender thread. She raised her hips to pull him in deeper. "You're killing me."

He could say the same. She'd turned out to be such a remarkable woman. In every way. He was pleased to have rekindled their friendship and that might've been enough, but now that he knew what she tasted like, he was hooked. "Sorry. I was a little too excited."

"By me?"

"Of course by you, you nutcase." He stole a kiss before he snapped his hips. Her eyes rolled back in her head, which was a good sign. He was going to stop thinking. It wasn't doing him any favors. All he wanted was laid out before him. She panted and rolled her head on the pillow, urging him to move faster with clutching fingers on his back, his arms, wherever she could reach. He didn't even mind when she dug into a couple of tender mementos from his sparring match earlier that day.

"I'm not going to go faster," he said.

Her eyes flashed. "Why the hell not?"

Just for that, he stopped altogether. Fine, so he was in her to the hilt, which felt unbelievably good, but she seemed intent on milking him to death. Not a bad thing… if he wanted this over in a minute flat. "Stop that," he said, giving her his most serious frown.

She froze, her hands, her body, her muscles. "Stop what? What's wrong?"

He kissed her nose. "You were squeezing."

Her arms hit the mattress. "Really? I wasn't trying to—"

"Not with your hands. Or your legs. Or anything on the outside."

"What, a test? Now?"

She made him laugh again. "Fine. Your internal muscles were making it very difficult to take things slowly."

"You're very obsessed with this slowly business." Her frown was just as serious as his had been. "Is it because I didn't want more foreplay?"

He laughed so hard he couldn't believe he was still inside her. "I'm fine about the foreplay."

"For a man your age?"

"For anyone over twenty-one."

"Oh. Well, then, what's the problem?"

He shook his head and pulled out slowly. Until only his tip was inside her. Then he thrust hard.

She cried out so loudly the people down the block must have heard.

"I apologize," he said. "About the whole slowly business. How about we take this from the top and go full throttle?"

Her inner muscles squeezed so hard he was the one crying out, "Oh, Christ."

"I'm more motivated by tech references," she said, her voice shaky from all the gasping, "but if you want engines revving, I can deal with that."

"Tell you what. You take the wheel. Tell me what you—"

She squeezed again. "That thing where I had to stop us from going through the headboard was pretty nifty."

He always had been good at following clear directions.

MATT HAD BOTH her legs up close to her chest and he was doing just what she'd asked him to. For a gloriously long time she'd been completely present, but his finger, slowly rubbing her between them, was making it harder to concentrate. She looked at him for the hundredth time, expecting his eyes to be closed or at least looking at something other than her. But no. They locked gazes, and it happened again. In addition to all the incredible things she felt, now her heart got into the mix.

All she knew for sure was that this was a gift. A rare opportunity. A once-in-a-lifetime reunion with benefits.

"I'm almost there," she said.

"Thank God," he said, the raspy sound of his voice making her chest feel even tighter. "I don't think I can hold out much longer."

"Don't. I want to watch."

He moaned and dropped his head a little. "No, I want you to—"

He rubbed her faster.

"No fair," she said, but she didn't really mean it. It had begun in earnest. The shivery moment on the brink, between knowing and abandoning thought. She wanted it to last forever.

"Come for me," he whispered.

That was it. The final push. She came spectacularly. The stars on the ceiling were nothing compared to the ones behind her eyelids. The aftershocks tumbled through her, and somewhere along the way, he'd come, and she'd seen the stretched muscles of his neck once more, the look of pleasure so close to pain.

When he flopped next to her, she was still trying to regain her breath, to come down from the orgasmic high. Not that she was anxious to return to reality. "Wow," she said. "As far as reunions with benefits go, this was the best one ever."

His panting stopped long enough for her to turn her head. His eyebrows dipped in a frown. "You've had a lot of those?"

"What?"

"Reunions with benefits?"

"Nope. Just this one."

He went back to looking smugly happy. "Good."

"The whole thing was planned, right? The massages, getting all naked and oily?"

"Hoped for, not planned. I was prepared for anything."

"Really?"

His hand found hers by groping around. "I'm sure I would've lived if you'd passed. But I'm glad you didn't."

Sam grinned, shutting out the niggling worry that teased at the back of her mind.

"So, has there been anyone?" he asked.

"I wasn't a virgin, if that's what you mean."

"I meant anyone special."

"Oh. No. Not really. Well, there was Ron. He's an

app-writer-turned-mogul. Lives in Silicon Valley now. We liked each other but obviously not enough to do anything about it."

"How did you meet?"

"At a party, if you can believe that. Ron was there, and I'd been hooked on his free game. I spent a fortune on his extras, and what started as me giving him a piece of my mind turned into a fun night."

"I'm sorry he doesn't live closer."

She shrugged. "It's easier, to be honest. I love the job so much I don't give much thought to dating. Although seeing Logan so happy with Kensey and knowing Rick met Jenna here while staying in the apartment made me wonder if there was something in the water here. So better watch it." She suddenly realized how that might sound and wanted to just die. "Plus," she said quickly, "I got a real live girlfriend out of the deal. Kensey is awesome."

"That's right. I never did see you with any girlfriends back at school."

"Most of my classes were filled with dudes."

He turned onto his side, resting his head on his hand. He looked really good. His hair was just a little damp, his dark eyes warm, his smile easy. "I think the word you're looking for is *geeks*."

"Or *nerds*. Either is correct, and I'm not ashamed of it. We are a passionate bunch."

"I'll say. I need to—" He looked toward the bathroom. After a brief surprise kiss, he stood up. All gorgeous and nude. His abs were almost a six-pack, which made her want to run her hands over them again. She'd always liked his body, and now that she had the complete picture, she liked it even more.

"Hey, speaking of parties, how would you like to come

with me to the gala on Saturday? It's the annual family fund-raiser." He paused, waiting for her to say something, probably, but she couldn't think of how to respond. "Anyway, I'd really like you to go with me, although, you know, if you can't, that's okay."

He turned then, and while she should have been busy ogling his naked butt, she was tripping over his request. Her? Be his date for the Wilkinson Annual Gala? Where she'd have to mingle? And dress up? Was he insane?

She busied herself with pulling up the bedding, even though it wasn't cold in the room. The walls were just walls once more, pale blue ones. The ceiling, though, was still full of stars, which was its nighttime default. She'd done the same thing at her house.

After sliding under the blankets, she thought again about his invitation. Why didn't he have a date already? she wondered. His ex was a big-time model. She imagined his life was full of stunning, smart women. The kind who went to galas the way she went to Burger King.

She didn't even have anything to wear. Two days' notice? What the hell was that?

She couldn't believe she was contemplating saying maybe. Even saying yes? But damn, it was bad enough going to tech conventions, where everyone spoke the same language. Going to a charity gala with a bunch of high-society people? She imagined there would probably be an orchestra. It was so, so beyond her realm. Whenever she'd been invited to anything gala-ish, she sent a check. Simple. This? Not so much.

Matt walked out of the bathroom, looking like a movie-star athlete playboy.

"Will there be an orchestra?"

He stalled on his way back to bed. "Yep. It's a gala.

There's dinner and dancing and a lot of obligatory small talk. But if you're there, at least I'd have someone I wanted to talk with. It would make the night more pleasant for me. But again, I'll understand if you don't want to go."

"Why don't you have a date?"

His half grin told her that her question wasn't exactly delicate. Before he answered, he got under the covers and scooched up next to her. "Because," he said, "I'm not seeing anyone, obviously."

"How is that obvious?"

He drew his head back and looked at her with disappointment on his face. "Because I'm in bed with you. Would I be here if I was involved in a relationship?"

"Oh. Right." She felt like a dope.

"Glad you think so highly of me."

She shook her head, hating that he actually looked hurt. "I wasn't thinking, okay? I just remember you from, you know, back in your glory days. There seemed to be a pretty steady stream of cheerleaders in your life."

"They weren't all cheerleaders. And I was a young punk. A very horny one. Besides, Rick and Logan weren't exactly monks."

She laughed. "No, they weren't, but in terms of sheer numbers, you came out ahead."

"I'm not ashamed of it. They were all perfectly nice women, and I never lied to a single one of them."

"I didn't think you would. Despite the odds, you're a nice guy."

"The odds?"

"Good-looking. Rich. Smart. Fit. You've got it all. You're a perfect package."

He put his hand on his junk over the bedding. "Thank you."

"Ha-ha. Right. That sense of humor of yours took away a few points but my statement still stands."

"No, I try to be. Nice, I mean. The Wilkinsons are raised to be conscientious and responsible... That is, when some, who won't be mentioned by name, aren't shopping." They both laughed. "Seriously," he said. "I'm thankful for the way I was raised."

"Yeah, you were lucky. And yes."

"Excuse me?"

"Yes," she repeated, shocking the hell out of herself. "I'll go to your fancy-ass party. With you."

The way his eyes lit up filled her with a warm gush of pleasure.

"Thanks, Sam. Now I'm not dreading it."

"Yeah, but you know how I am with people."

"You'll be with me. You don't have to talk to anyone else."

"Good."

"You sure?"

She rolled her eyes despite being so utterly unsure about this whole proposition it wasn't even funny.

His thank-you kiss was sweet and could have been trouble if she hadn't had a bellyful of panic.

Matt seemed put out when she told him she had to go home, but it was for the best. She probably wouldn't get any sleep in her own bed, but she had to try, considering all the work she had piling up in the lab. And now she had to figure out what she was going to wear to the gala.

Matt might be a prince of industry, but she was definitely not Cinderella.

9

SLUMPED IN HER CHAIR, Sam stared at the monitor. All the beautiful women in their beautiful dresses with their polite smiles made her sick to her stomach. Literally. It wasn't like the flu, but her insides were definitely wonky. That was what she got for doing a Google search of past Wilkinson galas. Everyone looked so polished and at ease. Didn't any of these people have social anxiety?

For all she knew, they did but hid it for the pictures. Hopefully, she wouldn't be in any, because she was certain her discomfort would be written all over her face.

Although, if Matt really did what he promised and stayed by her side, she should be okay. Thinking of Matt and the things they'd done last night dropped her into a different state altogether. If she didn't control her random smiles, Clark was going to start grilling her. And that most definitely wouldn't end well.

Her Spidey senses told her that he was glaring at her again, so she quickly minimized the picture on her computer screen so only her work was visible. The drawings needed to be completed for a meeting tonight. Completed and sent to Macrotech so they could give her their notes. This was the last pass for this baby before production.

It was a great new design on a USB-sized fully capable computer. So complete you could plug it into any port-equipped TV and there it would be. All thirty-two gigs of storage and two gigs of memory.

The project consumed her until the middle of rechecking the processor, when she thought of Matt again.

Of Matt naked. In bed. Leaning over her, looking into her eyes as he entered her.

Naturally, she blushed with all the subtlety of a fire hydrant and, of course, Clark chose that moment to look at her. Maybe he was always looking at her so she'd never get away with an errant thought.

There was nothing errant about Matt. Or the flashes of memories stored in her personal hard drive of a brain. She just wished there were some way to stop blushes before they started.

She instantly hit up Evernote and wrote "End to Blushing" for future study, then finished her review. Almost two hours had passed since she'd thought of the gala, and just noting that fact made her stomach rumble. Coffee would help. Coffee helped everything.

She walked by Tina's desk on her way to their break room. Tina was deep into her crash course on the 3-D printer, which made Sam so jealous she could spit, but that was one of the main reasons why Tina had been hired. She didn't look up, buried in the instruction manual. Odd. Clark's avatar of Obi-Wan Kenobi had migrated to the top right corner of Tina's desk. He never let Sam touch it. To be fair, she didn't let him touch her sacred Hermione Granger. Then her phone rang and she was off.

Once she'd finished her call, she slipped into the break

room. Sam set the fancy espresso machine to make her a double-shot hazelnut latte. Then she called her friend Kensey. Sam had met her when Logan was staying at the smart apartment. Kensey worked for one of Sam's earliest supporters, someone who'd put up a lot of money betting Sam would be a success. So when he mentioned his assistant was coming to Boston to attend a security conference, Sam had offered up the apartment.

Sam had come to really like Kensey, and their relationship had continued to develop.

By the time Sam had explained the situation with the black-tie affair and her wardrobe conundrum—complete with hyperlinks to photos from the past five galas—Kensey was way more excited about the whole thing than Sam was.

"Logan told me about Matt," Kensey said. "And I saw a picture of him. He's gorgeous."

"I know." Sam thought about running home, where she could Skype the call from the wall in private, but this had to be quick.

"Sexy, too," Kensey said.

"I know."

"And single."

"Oh, shut up. It's not like that," she said, which made Kensey laugh. "I want to look nice, you know, just fit in."

"Got it. I'll be in Boston tomorrow morning by—"

"What? No. That's crazy. Just look over the stuff I sent you and point me in the right direction."

Kensey laughed again. "Do you have any idea how many links and pictures you sent? Trust me, it'll be easier for me to take a commuter flight and do this in person," Kensey said. "You need to be in your best underwear by ten so we can hit the shops."

"My best underwear?"

After a long silent moment, Kensey said, "If we need to start there, you'd better be ready by nine. There's a seven-thirty flight, which means I can meet you for coffee at Au Bon Pain at Copley Place at nine thirty on the dot. We'll go to Intimacy at ten, and once you have the right bra and stuff, we'll go check out the designer gowns."

"Are you insane?"

"Somewhat. But I don't have anything too important going on tomorrow, and anyway, Logan is tied up with a new case."

"This just keeps getting worse. Kensey—"

"Come on—it'll be fun. And it just so happens I know a lot about dressing for galas."

Sam hadn't wanted a fuss. But she was over a barrel. Besides, seeing Kensey would be great. "I'll pay for your plane ticket."

"Just be ready. We have a lot to do. And stop freaking out. We'll make everything perfect, including your makeup and hair."

Sam hadn't even thought about makeup or hair. "Thanks," she said, then put her phone in her jeans pocket and drank her tepid latte in four big gulps.

Maybe Clark had a point about all this Matt stuff. Somehow her old college friend had managed to turn her world upside down in less than a week.

IT LOOKED LIKE a warehouse from the outside, but above the door was an elegantly crafted metal SOC. Matt rang the bell, knowing he could be sent away, but dammit, he wanted to see Sam. It had bothered him when she left last night. Since his divorce he'd had a few hookups and he'd always left the hotel room or her apartment. No big deal. Sleeping with a stranger was never comfortable. But Sam wasn't a stranger. He'd assumed she'd stay.

The door opened electronically. And there she was, both eyebrows raised to the limit, a question on her lips.

"I'll turn around right now if I'm interrupting something important. I was in the area, and I hadn't seen the place, so I took a chance. Probably should have called, though."

"If the only reason you came was to see the lab, then—"

He smiled as he crossed the threshold. "You know perfectly well I came to see you. I can't stop thinking about you. It's very inconvenient."

"Tell me about it," she muttered, sweeping a nervous glance to her right.

He wanted to pull her into a kiss, but this was her workplace and it wasn't cool to take liberties given the circumstances.

"I would have told you not to come," she said. "But now that you're here, I can show you around if you like. It's got to be speedy, though."

"Really? You won't hurt my feelings if you tell me to get lost."

She stepped aside, smiling shyly. "Come on in."

She smelled like coconut, her hair up in some kind of loose swirl. He liked that she was in jeans and a Nerdist T-shirt. Knowing what was under that shirt was even better. Jesus, maybe he could take her outside for five minutes. It wouldn't be enough, but he'd feel better having kissed her.

"This is the creative team work area," she said, pointing out the four desks, several drafting tables, walls of books, and bigger monitors than he'd ever seen. There was a young blonde woman Matt didn't know, and there was Clark. Who clearly did not approve of Matt showing up like this.

"You remember Clark," she said.

He walked over and held out his hand. He remembered Clark very well, but Matt didn't understand the hostility in his eyes. "Good to see you again," Matt said. "It's great how well you and Sam have done. Congratulations."

"Yeah, thanks." Clark had ended the handshake abruptly and was already sitting down. After what looked like a warning to Sam, he went back to his work.

Sam didn't seem put out by Clark's behavior, which was strange. But Matt let it go as she moved him along past a massive printer and a small kitchen dominated by an espresso machine. Everywhere he looked, there were things stuck on the wall: pictures of characters from online games and photos of everything from dragons to the Mars rover. "Is that a massage chair?" he asked, noticing the distinctive-looking chair sitting off by itself away from any desks.

"It is. We also have a treadmill." She pointed to the other side of the huge space. "We're always hunched over a machine. The massage helps."

He stepped closer and brushed a speck of nothing off her cheek. The touch was like a gateway drug, and he pulled her into his arms. "As good as last night's?"

Sam blushed. "Not even close."

"This is a very cool office," he said. "I'm jealous. Mine is boring. I have no dragon pictures whatsoever."

Her smile was genuine and her gaze full of fire. She touched his arm, two fingers. "I can't stop thinking," she said, "about, you know. And the gala…"

Goddamn, he wanted her. But instead of dragging

her into the break room, locking the door and taking her on the little round table inside, he put some distance between them.

"Hey, um, I was wondering. When you left last night—"

"Sorry to interrupt—" Clark's voice barged in like a battering ram "—but I need to know if we're going to make that eight o'clock deadline. If not, I'll have to—"

"We are going to make it. Matt's only here for a quick tour, and we're almost done. Give me a minute, okay?"

"Fine." Clark met Matt's eye. "Sorry about this, but we're on killer schedules. Sam's work is demanding. Everyone wants a piece of her."

"Right," Matt said, wondering if Clark was intentionally trying to bait him with that last line. "Don't worry. I won't keep her for long."

Clark, who still looked like the beefy kid he'd been back in college, opened his mouth as if to make another comment, then closed it again, nodded and left.

"Sorry. I really shouldn't have come today."

Sam didn't respond except to lead him back through the lab until they both stepped outside. All she truly wanted to do was take him back to her house, lock the doors and screw like bunnies until the day after tomorrow. No gala, no shopping, no angry Clark. But she had responsibilities. Taking off tomorrow meant she had to work like a demon for the rest of the day.

Matt took her hand in his. "I was thinking maybe after work, I could see where you live."

"Oh, no. It's a mess. I wouldn't want you to see it. As it is, I'm going to do everything I can to be at the apartment by eight o'clock. If that's okay."

"If? Are you kidding? It would be great. And you could stay—"

She shook her head. She'd hoped he wouldn't bring it up. Staying overnight would not be a good idea. Hell, just seeing him tonight was nuts. But her chances to be with him were finite. "I don't think I can. I don't tend to sleep well with other people, and I'm meeting Kensey at nine thirty tomorrow to shop for a dress."

He nodded as he leaned in and kissed her. And it was only after his hand started moving lower down her back that she remembered the camera above the door.

If Clark hadn't got the picture before, he would now.

Sam stepped back, breaking the connection she hadn't wanted to lose. "I'll see you tonight," she said.

CLARK WAS STARING at her again. Disapproval dripping from his every pore. She'd had enough. Saving her work, she got up and went to his desk. "What the hell, Clark? Why are you so moody? Did Matt do something to you in college? Is that why you hate him?"

"I don't hate him. The work—"

"We talked about this. I'm sorry I'm messing up the timetables, but come on. I'm not working tomorrow at all, because I'm going to the Wilkinson Gala. And if it runs late, I'm probably not going to make it in on Sunday. But Matt will be gone soon, and everything will go back to normal."

He snorted. "You sure about that?"

"What?"

Clark stood up and crossed his arms over his chest, but he didn't look at her. "Just, I remember how hard you crushed on Matt back at MIT. And now you drop everything for the guy—who doesn't even live in Boston, I might add. When he leaves, the odds of you seeing him again are pretty low."

"Gee, it seems you've had a lot of free time to snoop into my business." His words stung and she didn't care that he looked embarrassed. True, she wouldn't see much of Matt after this week, but she already knew that. She sure didn't need anyone else pointing it out. "I'm not six-teen anymore, Clark. Please don't treat me as if I am. I'm entitled to a life outside of this company."

He turned to look at her, and she could see concern behind the anger in his eyes. "I worry you'll end up get-ting hurt."

She tempered her reaction a little. "You're right—I did have a crush on Matt for a long time, but that was ages ago. When we were *all* kids. I've got this under control. Okay? You can count on me returning to base camp re-freshed and ready to rock. So please, just let this happen, all right? I know it's inconvenient about the work, but we can deal with that. As you pointed out, people want the stuff we make. They'll wait."

Clark nodded, then gave her the first smile she'd seen from him in ages.

"You know what?" she said. "You shouldn't work this weekend, either."

"Seriously? Someone's got to—"

"They'll wait."

He didn't respond immediately. When he did, he sounded like her best friend Clark. "Yeah, they will," he said. Then he headed for the break room while she wondered if she'd just lied to him. This wasn't like her crush back in school, and she had absolutely no illusions about a happily-ever-after. Those kinds of illusions were the reason she wasn't going to spend the night with him. Going to sleep would be fine. But waking up to Matt? No. She needed to hang on to the fact that this was vacation sex. Period.

The scary part was, her heart was already beating in a new rhythm. Good thing she was an expert at burying herself in her work at the expense of everything else. She'd be fine.

Assuming she could get through the shopping trip tomorrow. And the gala. She tried her best not to whimper.

MATT CHECKED THE time again. Almost 9:00 p.m. Sam hadn't called, which meant she was probably too busy to see him, and he should just get over it. Eat a burger, go to bed, beat off. The end. No drama necessary. He'd see her tomorrow—

The doorbell rang. Ten seconds later she was in his arms. Kissing him as if they'd just discovered how. Between the two of them, they somehow managed to get her coat off.

"Sorry," she said, pulling him down for another kiss. By the time they took a breather, about half their buttons and zippers were undone. Her hair thing was a casualty, and he stepped on her foot. Basically, they were going at it like animals.

And he couldn't get enough.

When he couldn't stand it another second, he grabbed two handfuls of her behind and lifted. She automatically put her legs around his waist, and he made damn good time carrying her to the bed.

"I'm sorry I'm late," she said, her lips red and pouty from all their kissing.

"Don't care. Too many clothes."

She yanked off her T and her cute white bra. He was already down to his boxer briefs but she caught up fast. For a moment, they just stared at each other. She seemed especially interested in his cock, which made him even harder.

Just as he was going to do something about the bedding, Sam took charge, ripping down the comforter as though it had done her wrong. Then she scooted onto the bed, jiggling in all the right places.

Taking full precautions, he put on a condom before he joined her. She straddled his waist and kissed him, leaning forward so that his head ended up on the pillow.

"Okay?" she asked, breathlessly.

"Anything you want."

She kissed him again as she rode him slow and steady, rubbing her erect nipples on his chest, then leaning back and sinking all the way down. Jesus.

A few minutes later—maybe to stop from coming, maybe just because he liked being on top—he flipped them, landing her safely on her back. With her legs around him, he found the perfect angle and, by some miracle, held off coming until she climaxed so hard his head hit the headboard.

Before she'd had her second aftershock, he'd come as hard as he could remember ever coming.

It took him ten minutes to realize the walls were scattered with images of a train entering a tunnel, a champagne cork popping, fountains spurting, fireworks, even a volcano erupting. The sound track? Bow-chika-bow-wow straight from the '70s.

It made him laugh so hard it hurt.

10

Somehow Sam found herself standing in front of a three-way mirror, Kensey on her right and a woman she didn't know cupping her breasts from behind.

"You see how you're held up beautifully with a perfect décolletage in this lovely demi bra. Depending on the dress, of course."

Sam just nodded. It felt as if everyone in the exclusive bra-fitting store had seen and/or touched her boobs. She'd got so used to it she wasn't even blushing anymore.

"We'll want one demi, one strapless, one PrimaDonna," Kensey said, gesturing as she spoke, "and we'd better throw in a couple of comfortable day sets, because honestly, Sam, where did you get the bra you're wearing today? Goodwill?"

Sam tried not to glare at her friend. She was trying to help, after all. "Can we please try to focus on the task at hand?" Sam asked, reevaluating the *joy* of having a female friend. "I liked that pink one, the teal one, the black and the beige and also this one."

"I think I know which ones you mean," LeCiel, the gorgeous fitter, said. "Why don't you keep that one on, since you know you want it, and give me a few minutes to get the rest together."

"Great," Kensey said, then turned to Sam. "Why don't you put on your T and let's step out for a moment. Not so many mirrors."

"Only my T-shirt?"

"It's long enough. Besides, there's that big wall in the middle of the store. No one's going to see you."

"Besides the staff and customers?"

"They're all used to women wearing much less. Besides, you look beautiful. I'd say just wear that to the party if we can't find the right dress," Kensey said and held the door open for her.

"You could have warned me that I'd be felt up."

Kensey grinned. "These people are professionals. Their job is making you look beautiful, and I'd say they succeeded. Besides, you had a front-row seat while I met Logan for the first time wearing a towel."

"You looked fantastic in that towel. I'm not you."

"I'd tell you to put on your big-girl panties, but you were already wearing them. The ones you've got on now, though, they look sensational."

What they were was small. Looking both ways to see if anyone else was around, Sam reluctantly stepped out of the dressing room.

The area behind the wall was as stunning as the rest of the shop. Sexy underwear was the only art on the walls, all colors, all kinds. It was unnerving, and Sam had to fight the urge to cover herself even though the T-shirt really wasn't all that revealing.

"So, tell me more about Matt."

For someone who'd flown in to Boston first thing this morning, Kensey looked unfairly relaxed and beautiful.

Her blond hair rested on her shoulders, and she wore black skinny jeans with a perfectly starched white blouse. Together with her ballet flats, she looked very Audrey Hepburn. Sam admired Kensey's style, which was why she'd turned to her for help in the first place. If Sam ever got it together to have a personal style, she'd want one like Kensey's. "What else do you want to know?"

Kensey tsked. "Everything. I know he's gorgeous, et cetera, but I want to know what it's like seeing him after so long. I know you two hadn't corresponded for quite a while."

"He's great. And we've been, you know, catching up."

"Really?"

Sam shrugged. "We're just friends."

"So Logan said." Kensey tilted her head to the side and studied Sam. "Somehow I got a different impression."

Without saying a word, Sam let her know she was right with the heat filling her cheeks.

"I'm a blusher, too." Kensey waved dismissively. "Lucky you, it just makes you more alluring."

"Yeah. Alluring is exactly how I feel when I'm beet red."

It didn't take long for them to pick out seven everyday bras, all with matching panties. One was a thong, which went against Sam's principles, but she had to admit she looked kind of sexy in it.

Then they were off to Neiman Marcus for more shopping torture.

"Come on, Sam. This shouldn't be a burden. It's a brand-new experience. Think of it as putting together a cosplay costume. Where you're the strong, successful heroine that the hero needs to win. Buffy in a designer gown."

Sam stopped suddenly, and a boy who'd been walking behind her ran into her. But he didn't hit her nearly as hard as the realization that she was being a horrible person. "You're right. I've done cosplay and I enjoy it. Thanks, and I'm sorry."

"Stop it," Kensey said, taking her hand. "I just want you to have more fun."

"You flew all the way from New York and all I've been doing is complaining."

"It wasn't a hardship. I wanted to be here. Come on. I still have a hundred questions about you and Matt."

"Oh, good, my second-favorite part of the day."

Kensey slowed. "I thought this was what girlfriends were supposed to do."

"Supposed to?" Sam said, and then she remembered Kensey's difficult past. Her nontraditional upbringing had left her on shaky ground, but you'd never guess by looking at her. "I'm not good at this, either," Sam admitted. "But I want to be. Although I'm not really comfortable talking about sex."

Kensey's lips curved in a patient smile. "So tell me something else about Matt and you."

"All right. I slept with him the night I turned sixteen."

Kensey burst out laughing, then immediately sobered up, her eyes as big as silver dollars. "Uh…"

Sam laughed and pulled her friend into the high-end department store, where they headed to the escalator to go to the third floor. "Nothing happened. Trust me. Except…and you have to promise not to tell Logan, okay?"

"You bet. Not a word. Except what?"

"He kissed me," Sam said, remembering the thrill of that night. "It was my first."

"Oh, wow. Then this—"

"This," Sam said, "is a hookup. Nothing more. Well, we're friends, so it matters, but a hookup is all it is. I'm sure the way I feel about him has way more to do with my teen crush than the man he is now."

They arrived at the women's couture section. "We're going to find you a dress," Kensey said. "Then we're going to break for a quick bite and you're going to tell me everything. Got it?"

"Not everything."

"I didn't mean that like it sounded."

"I know." They both laughed. It was kind of crazy, the two of them trying to navigate a friendship like a pair of teenagers. "That sounds good— Hold on." A color caught Sam's eye.

She wasn't sure what designer the dress was by but the color, though… She steered Kensey toward the gown. It was a brilliant teal, strapless with a tight ribboned bodice, crystal embroidery over the waist and a chiffon skirt. "I want to try this one."

Like magic, someone from the store was walking toward them that very minute.

"It will look amazing with your hair," the smartly dressed sales associate said. "You're a size zero?"

"Two, unless they run big, which I can't imagine."

"I'll bring it to you in the fitting room, along with a few others by the same designer."

She led them to a mirrored suite. Before she left to gather the gowns, Kensey said, "My friend is going to the Wilkinson Gala tonight. She needs shoes, nails, makeup and hair all by what…?"

"Six-ish?"

"Six-ish," Kensey said, taking over, much to Sam's

delight. "I'm from New York. She doesn't shop. So, can you help?"

The woman—Taylor, according to the tag on her blazer—was looking at them as if they'd just arrived from another planet. "The gala is tonight."

"Yes—hard to believe but true." Kensey held on to a smile. "Can you help us?"

"Yes, of course," the woman said, but she was clearly rattled, which didn't help Sam's nerves at all. "What's your shoe size?"

"Eight narrow," Sam said. "And not too high, because I'll fall down."

Taylor seemed at a bit of a loss. She blinked at Sam and then smiled. "Yes, of course, not too high. Perhaps I should alert the tailor, as well. Also, the salon here is quite nice, but if you have a favorite—"

"The salon here sounds perfect." Sam liked the idea of not having to go anywhere else.

"Wonderful," Taylor said. "I can set up an appointment for you after we're done here, if that suits you?" Sam nodded. "I'll just go find those gowns for you now." And with that, Sam's fairy godmother was off, leaving her and Kensey alone in the giant dressing room.

"I'm never going to be ready in time," Sam moaned, shaking her head.

"Yes, you will. We're already halfway there."

"You're not very good at math, are you?"

Kensey laughed. "Okay," she said, sitting on a cushioned bench. "While you undress, tell me three words that describe Matt when you were in college together."

"Easy," she said, once again taking off her blue button-down. "Smart, funny and, um, honorable."

Kensey opened her mouth, but Sam cut her off. "Wait.

Kind. I should have said kind. And sincere." She unbuttoned her Levi's 501s but didn't push them down. "He was honest as could be. I don't have to say handsome, because, well… But he was a gentleman, even when he was drunk. Also a scholar. You know he was the editor of the *Harvard Law Review* when he was in his second year of law school? That's more than three words," Sam said. "But he was patient, too. And generous."

"So, Prince Charming?"

"Oh, he could also be a dick. Wasn't a good loser at all. But maybe that was because we mostly played computer games when we were together and I tended to win every time."

"Glad to hear he's human." Kensey smiled. "To tell you the truth, I was sold on Matt the minute Logan told me about him covering the rent so you guys could keep the house you lived in back in college."

Sam frowned. She had no idea what Kensey was talking about.

"I mean, come on. How many twenty-year-old guys would think of doing something that generous? You need to add 'thoughtful' to that list."

Sam was totally confused. She and the guys had shared a house their junior and senior years. Well, minus Logan. The army had stolen him away the summer before his last year at MIT. "I honestly don't know what you mean."

It was Kensey's turn to frown. "Huh. Maybe Logan was the only one who knew about it at the time." She sighed. "I guess it doesn't matter at this point, but I'd prefer you didn't mention to Logan that I told you."

"I don't get it," Sam said.

"Logan's and Matt's names were on the lease. After Logan left for the army, in order for all of you to stay in the house, Matt made up Logan's share of the rent. Otherwise you and Rick wouldn't have been able to afford to live there. But Matt didn't want you guys to know."

For a genius, Sam was pretty stupid. She should have figured out that someone had helped subsidize her share of the rent all those years ago. Well, she was never going to make fun of anyone else's math again. "I didn't know…"

"Of course you didn't." Kensey's lips lifted in a wry smile. "Not until I opened my big mouth."

"I won't say anything to Logan or Matt."

"Thank you. Although, I'm sure I'll end up confessing to Logan myself. We're both working at not keeping secrets from each other." She didn't have to say more. Sam understood that Kensey had been shrouded in mystery most of her life and was trying to overcome that. "I was going to ask you to tell me three words to describe the Matt you know now, but I guess I don't have to…"

Sam stilled. Opened her mouth and then shut it. She smiled and slowly shook her head. She'd always thought Matt was an amazing person. What she'd learned a minute ago was just more proof.

"Look," Kensey said, her voice serious, "I'm just saying, try to keep an open mind. Don't rule him out yet. And maybe don't label this reunion as *just* anything. Lots can happen in a short time. Trust me. I held myself back from Logan, believing, beyond a doubt, that we could never be together. I almost lost him. If I had, it would have been the biggest mistake of my life."

Sam took in what Kensey said, but before they could talk more, the teal dress arrived. Along with four other stunning gowns. "Oh, for God's sake, all the gowns I love don't even need bras," Sam exclaimed.

From that moment on, it was all *Pretty Woman* for the rest of the afternoon. All the fussing and attention almost made Sam forget where she was going that night.

But not whom she was going with.

MATT GOT SETTLED in the back of the hotel limo. It had come with a bottle of champagne but also the scotch he preferred. The advantage of being a Wilkinson. He didn't like playing the family card, but he'd planned on going to the gala solo, in a cab, and that wouldn't do for Sam.

It was amazing that she'd agreed to this. He'd thought about letting her off the hook, but then he found out that Kensey was flying in, and he figured he'd leave it be. It might just have been selfishness on his part, but the idea of Sam sitting next to him at yet another party full of rich people who wanted to network made him very happy.

The last sip of Glenfiddich went down as smoothly as the first, the hint of cinnamon blossoming in his chest. He'd poured only a small glass of the stuff. It was more important to share a glass of champagne with Sam.

She'd called him at a little after five to ask him to pick her up at the lab. They were almost there. Damn if his pulse didn't speed up, and it definitely wasn't because of the single malt.

The limo pulled up in front of Sam's building, and the chauffeur started to get out of the car. "Bill, I'll just get out, but I think my friend would like it if you opened the door for her."

His chauffeur nodded respectfully. "Sure thing, Mr. Wilkinson."

The path to the doorway looked very different at night. He knew the lights were all about security, but they were artfully placed. When he rang the bell, he took a couple of steps back, wanting to get the full impression of Sam all dressed up.

He was unprepared.

She looked like a 1940s movie star, her red hair parted on one side, cascading in lush curls past her shoulder. The dress was something else. Pure white and covered with crystals or sequins on top but with a slit down the center that showcased her perfect pale skin and just a hint of the breasts he knew very well.

The bottom was all silky and sheer, really sheer. He could see her thighs, those fantastic legs, but the whole package was elegant as hell.

"You're a showstopper," he said, trying hard not to just let his jaw drop and stare. "You look so beautiful."

She turned around, and the back view was just as arresting. When she faced him again, it was with her familiar blush. "You think I'll fit in?"

"No way," he said, moving in to steal a kiss. "You'll be the most stunning woman in the room."

"Right," she said. "I'm a lot of things, but the belle of the ball isn't one of them."

He pulled her close. "You are to me," he said, then kissed her fresh pink lips.

When she pulled back, he was reluctant to let go. "You know we don't have to go to the gala. We could just go back to the apartment. Let me find out how to take off this sensational dress."

"Are you kidding? Do you have any idea what it took to get me looking like this? We're going."

He laughed, but part of him had been serious.

Escorting her to the car meant walking slowly. The pavers weren't all that even and she was in heels. Bill opened the door and held it for her as if she were royalty.

"This is quite fancy," she said when they were both seated and on their way. "Champagne?"

"Would you like some?"

"Sure."

He uncorked the bottle, and she asked, "Tell me more about the fund-raiser. I know it's for the Boston Children's Hospital, and I'm very impressed with that, but why did you guys choose it?"

"My great-grandfather was born with a heart problem. They fixed him up, and from that time on, the family has hosted a fund-raising gala. Most of Boston's elite will be there. We'll see a few politicians, some lobbyists, lots of rich people." He poured her a glass and waited until she took a sip before he poured his own.

"That's very cool. I didn't know it had a personal connection." She used her free hand to pull up a tiny silver purse. From it, she took out a check. "I want to make a donation, but usually my accountant handles that. So, is there, like, a donation jar at the party or something?"

He nearly spilled his drink as a laugh burst out of him. "Nope, no jar. But how about I take care of it for you?"

"That's fine," she said, handing it to him.

He nearly spilled his drink again when he saw the check was drawn for half a million dollars. "Sam. This is a hell of a donation. Are you—"

"Of course I'm sure. It's a great hospital. They do wonderful things."

"You'll make my mother's night."

"Okay. Remember, you promised to stick with me. Especially when we're meeting your family."

"I promised, and I will. It's so boring doing all the

expected schmoozing, but with you there? Well, let's just say this promises to be the best gala I've ever attended."

Sam smiled and downed her champagne in one big gulp.

11

It took Sam a while to get over Matt's reaction to seeing her at the lab. The security lighting had made it very easy to see his eyes, and she truly believed he was telling her the truth. That to him, she was beautiful.

Her appearance hadn't been something she'd ever paid much attention to. Too many other things interested her. But like most little girls, she'd read fairy tales, and besides Matt, she'd had a couple of other crushes on guys—mostly movie stars—so nights like this were stored in her hard drive, but they weren't anything *real*.

Of course, he looked like a dream in his tuxedo. He would have looked at home on any magazine cover. All that handsome in one place. It was no surprise that people stared at him. He was better-looking than anyone else she had ever seen, and he was a Wilkinson, after all. And she knew he was the company's senior counsel, but she had no idea what it meant to be part of a dynasty.

The gala was in the main ballroom, and it was like walking into another world. Sam wasn't a total rube. Before she'd started sending checks to worthy causes, she'd been to a few fund-raisers, but nothing on this scale. This was extravagant squared. The orchestra was very large, larger than most ballrooms could accommodate. Above the musicians hung a large-screen monitor playing a continuous slide show of hospital promo pics. All around them were round tables, with fall-themed centerpieces. There were the ubiquitous white-jacketed waiters and waitresses carrying trays of champagne, but there were also strategically placed cocktail stations. Made sense if your goal was to raise money. Get 'em wasted and go for the big bucks.

They hadn't made it very far into the room when the first couple approached them. The man was older than the woman by at least one wife, and he looked Sam over as if she were a brand-new car.

"Matthew," the man said, holding out his hand. "Good to see you. We only seem to connect at these parties, don't we?"

Matt was very cordial. Introduced her with her full name. The husband, Culver Gordon, didn't offer Sam his hand. "I'm a lobbyist," he said. "American Hospital Association."

"I didn't realize hospitals had lobbyists."

The wife, Georgia, added, with a slight eyeroll, "Everything's got lobbyists."

"I suppose so."

"Sam's in computers," Matt said, which was accurate.

"Oh, I just got one of those Apple Watches," Georgia said, "but I can't seem to do anything but tell the time on it."

Sam smiled. "I know. I swear you need an advanced degree to figure them out."

Georgia smiled and nodded.

"I hope you two have a wonderful evening," Matt said.

"We'd stay and talk, but I haven't even said hello to the folks yet." His arm hadn't left its place around her shoulders, and Sam beamed inwardly at the thought.

They continued on their way through the room, being stopped every few paces. It was ridiculous how many people Matt knew. It had literally taken them ten minutes to make it a few feet. He knew most of the guests, at least by name, but had to be reminded of one couple's last name in order to introduce Sam.

She could see it had embarrassed him, so when the same look flickered on his face the next time, Sam took control of the situation. "Hi, I'm Sam O'Connel," she said, extending her hand to the woman.

"Toni Baxter. This is my husband, Alan."

When they were done making small talk, Matt squeezed her close. "What happened to that socially challenged girl I used to know? That was a slick move. How'd you know I couldn't remember her name?"

"You have a tell, Mr. Wilkinson," she whispered close to his ear. "I would advise you to stay away from poker tables."

He brushed her earlobe with his lips. "Great save. You really have come a long way."

"Okay, but you can't do that anymore."

Matt smiled. He didn't ask what she meant. The shiver must've been her tell.

As they moved on, she thought about what Matt had said. Jumping in as she had was not her way. Maybe Matt was right and she had changed a lot since college. Or maybe she was simply willing to do just about anything for Matt. The thought unnerved her.

Finally, they got close enough to get champagne, but also for Matt to point out his parents. Mr. Wilkinson was a good-looking-enough man—tall and lean, with perfectly trimmed silver hair. But Matt's mother was beautiful. She wore an elegant lavender gown and her dark hair was cut into a flattering bob. What Sam noticed most about her was her smile, which was easy and gracious.

Matt's sister was there, too, sheathed in a long red gown with her dark hair swept up. Not surprisingly, she was stunning, also.

Sam watched his family members moving through the crowd as easily as she wandered through a Best Buy, making nice with everyone.

"Those are my uncles, Frank and Peter." Matt pointed out two older men who were standing apart from the big crowd. They were having a private conversation and looked very serious.

"Your father's brothers?"

"Yep. They're also board members. I need a real drink—how about you?"

"I could do with a martini. I should also have an elegant cigarette holder and a lady pistol in my purse."

Matt winked at her. "You make a wicked-good dame."

Sam laughed as they headed for the nearest cocktail station. "You don't even talk like a real Bostonian. But you fake it well."

"Drummed out of me before it had a chance to take hold. Speaking of taking hold—incoming."

It was his parents. They were headed their way when someone who had a microphone announced that dinner would be served.

Sam's heart raced at the prospect of meeting Matt's parents. There was no reason to be so nervous, but she was.

"Samantha O'Connel," Matt said, his hand an anchor

on the small of her back. "May I introduce Charles and Bette Wilkinson, my parents."

Sam nodded. "Very nice to meet you."

They both smiled. "And you, as well," his mother said. "Tell me, Samantha, are you from Boston, or just here for the gala?"

"I live here," Sam said, sliding a glance at Matt, who was smiling at her. "I went to school with Matt and I've always wanted to tell you what a remarkable son you raised." She focused on his mother when she felt him shift beside her. He probably wanted her to shut up. Too bad. "Matt helped me a great deal when I was at MIT. I was very young and he became my protector and friend. I don't know what I would have done without him."

His mother frowned slightly. "All right, yes. I remember him speaking about you," Bette said. "He mentioned you were a prodigy."

"Yeah, that was me. The designation gets taken away as soon as you reach eighteen."

"Culver Gordon tells me that you've made quite a name for yourself." Matt's dad looked straight into her eyes. "He spoke very highly of your company. I'll have to look it up on the exchange."

"SOC is privately owned, but thanks."

"Dad, you're about to be called up to the dais," Matt said. "We'll catch up with you later, okay?"

"I look forward to it," Bette said. Her husband simply smiled and headed toward the orchestra area.

"You weirdo," Matt whispered. "You didn't have to say that to my folks."

"Yes, I did. They should know how terrific you are." She blushed when his arm tightened around her shoulders. "But I guess they already do."

Matt just kept smiling at her.

"What?"

"Have I told you how beautiful you look?" he whispered, his warm breath tickling her ear.

"About a thousand times. You should've warned me to bring a calculator and a bigger purse," she grumbled but couldn't stop smiling herself.

He laughed, and he might've kissed her hair—she wasn't sure—as he steered them toward the tables.

They found their assigned seats—Matt explained that the Wilkinsons were purposely spread out—and ordered drinks, and then the lights went down before they even had a chance to meet their tablemates.

Charles began his speech. It was more casual than Sam had expected but very earnest. He spoke of the family tradition, why they raised funds for the hospital—all the things she had expected.

When the lights came back on, the servers descended on the tables, and after they had received their first course—a Boston Bibb salad sprinkled with truffles—Matt started in on the introductions.

Among the others seated at their table were a distant cousin of Matt's and his wife and a woman named Kelly Sutter, who'd recently snagged a major security contract with the state. She recognized Sam from a presentation she'd done at a security conference earlier in the year.

Sam was used to being recognized at places like Comic-Con or the Consumer Electronics Show, but at a fund-raiser for a hospital? It was flattering and a little nerve-racking.

Kelly wanted to know more about Sam's inventions, and Sam answered her questions as the servers came around with their second course: bisque and lobster rolls. Talking to Kelly was easy; this was Sam's wheelhouse, and she was feeling surprisingly relaxed. But then Matt's cousin, who had seemed exceedingly bored by the conversation, said, "Matthew, isn't Sam too smart for you? I thought models and movie stars were more your speed."

"Actually," Sam said, putting down her fork and leaning forward, "Matthew and I met at MIT. He was Phi Beta Kappa. And when he went to Harvard Law, he was made editor of the *Law Review* when he was just a second-year—"

Matt put a hand on her thigh and whispered, "It's okay."

She smiled, holding back the rest of her objections to the guy's so-called joke. "I'm sorry. I suppose you already know all that. I just get carried away sometimes."

At least Rude Cousin looked a bit chastened. Across the table, Aaron something-or-other turned to his wife and said, "How come you never jump to my defense like that?" Everyone at the table laughed—except Rude Cousin—and Matt found her hand and gave it a squeeze.

Once dinner and the speeches were over, everyone went back to mingling, much as before. Matt was always within arm's reach. One of Matt's uncles was suddenly in front of Matt, looking at him with those serious eyes. He introduced himself, then asked Sam if he could steal Matt away for a moment.

"Are you sure we can't do this later?" Matt asked, his voice laced with that firm edge that had taken Sam by surprise when he'd been on the phone a few days earlier.

Uncle Frank shook his head. "It won't take long, I promise."

Matt turned to Sam. "I'm so sorry. I won't be gone longer than five minutes. Will you be all right?"

"Of course. Go. I'll just wait for the champagne to come by."

He kissed her briefly on the lips. "Five minutes."

Which gave her just enough time to scope out Vanessa, Matt's ex-wife. A wave of tension went through Sam as she watched Vanessa work the room. The woman was stunning. She was far more beautiful than anyone else in the room, her dress hugging her curves perfectly. Then Vanessa caught sight of Sam, and from the snooty once-over she gave her, it seemed she was aware that Sam was Matt's date.

It was easy to see that Vanessa didn't understand what Matt was doing with Sam, but that just made Sam stand taller and move closer to Matt when he returned to her side. Screw the ex.

Matt introduced Sam to his uncle Peter and Simon, another board member, and they were all standing around, sipping their drinks and making idle chitchat, when a man walked up to them.

"Excuse me, but are you Samantha O'Connel, the inventor?" he asked.

The other three people in their group stopped talking and stared, not at Sam but at the man speaking.

"That's me, yes," she said.

He held out his hand. "I'm Greg Hayes, CEO of Untied Technologies. My employees who attended the June security conference had a great many positive things to say about you. In fact, we placed a sizable order with your company, and so far, we've been very pleased. You're very, very clever, Ms. O'Connel. I'm just sorry you own your own company, or I'd steal you away. Maybe next year I'll attend the conference and come to hear your presentation."

"Thank you," she said. "I remember Walter and Toby." Because they were techies like her. "They were great.

But if I were you, I wouldn't bother coming to my presentation. To be honest, you probably wouldn't understand most of it." Oh, God.

Why hadn't she just stopped when she was ahead? But then Greg Hayes laughed. Pretty damn loud and hard. So did the rest of the group, including Matt and the members of the board. She breathed a sigh of relief.

"You're probably right," he said. "But I have a feeling it would be worth it just to see you in action."

"Well, then, good. We'll meet again."

"Could you excuse us for a moment?" Matt said, taking her hand. "I'm being summoned."

Their getaway was swift and filled with purpose. Matt led her straight past his folks to an alcove near the orchestra and the kitchen.

"I shouldn't have said what I did to Greg," Sam said, burying her face in her hands. "His company is in the Fortune 500."

"Come on—you were great. I didn't bring you here because I was angry. I just wanted to do this." His hands, so large and strong, skimmed under her hair to the nape of her neck as his thumbs caressed her face. A second later his mouth was on hers. He kissed her hard, passionately, possessively.

It made her knees weak. She wrapped her arms around his neck, and he put one hand on the small of her back and pulled her in tighter. They kissed as if there were no party around them, no orchestra. As if it were just the two of them.

Inevitably, a waitress interrupted their private moment. She clearly hadn't expected them, and they were just lucky she wasn't carrying a full tray as she nearly crashed into them. They stepped out of the alcove, and

Matt leaned down so he could whisper "Come dance with me" in her ear.

"I don't dance," she said.

"Please."

"They're all dancing the waltz or something. I don't know any of that stuff," Sam said, realizing too late she should have warned him before she agreed to come. "I bet you do, though."

"I do not."

"Liar. Isn't ballroom dancing part of those etiquette classes all rich kids have to take?"

He rolled his eyes at her. "Yes, okay, I know how. Come on, Sam. Do you trust me?"

"No. Not at all."

He grinned as he took her hand and brought her onto the dance floor. He lifted both her arms so they came around his shoulders; then he slid his hands behind her back. "This is easy, Sammy," he said, his voice warm and close. "Everyone knows the high school shuffle, right?"

She couldn't help but laugh. Yes, she'd done this at an excruciating party when she was twelve, but dancing with Matt was completely different. While everyone around them was doing fancy moves and impressive dips, she held on tighter and tighter until they were chest to chest, heart to heart, forehead to forehead, swaying in the corner to the sound of their own music.

It was the most perfect night ever.

12

THE MUSIC STOPPED, but Matt and Sam didn't, at least not right away. Finally, he reluctantly pulled back and said, "You about ready to leave?"

"I don't think the party's over." She glanced around at the crowd and gave him a pained look. "You want to leave because of my big mouth, don't you?"

"I hope you know I like you *because* you're insane, not in spite of it."

She wrinkled her nose. "Seriously, I was kind of rude to that CEO—"

"Sam, I do want to leave because of you, but not because of anything you've said." He moved away from their light embrace only to take her hand and bring it to his mouth. The scent of her skin had been driving him crazy since he'd whisked her away to the alcove. It was an extraordinary feeling to be with her like this. Yet another way of looking at his Sammy. She'd been utterly herself tonight, only dressed up like Cinderella.

"I'm not sure how long I can keep my hands off you. I want to be done with all this and put all my focus on making you come."

It never failed to amaze him that Sam's blush could go from zero to sixty in seconds. She swept a nervous gaze from her left to her right. He just smiled and waited for her response. Of course, he'd already made sure he couldn't be heard.

"I lied to your parents," she said. "Their son isn't so remarkable after all. He's a very wicked young man. Maybe I should go set them straight."

Her earnest-looking frown didn't worry him. Her sense of humor still made him grin. "Okay, we're definitely leaving," he said, taking her arm.

"Wait." She started laughing and tugged free. "You want me to fall on my butt? I'm not used to these skyscraper heels. Besides, I need to go to the restroom before we go."

"Would you like me to go with you, in case I have to catch that very delectable derriere?"

"No." She pointed to the bar near the exit. "I'll meet you there."

"Got it." He watched her walk away. The sheer fabric that swirled around her legs made it difficult for him to keep his composure. Too bad he couldn't have watched her from a distance while keeping her close. Both views were terrific.

She disappeared, and the first person Matt saw was his uncle Frank. Jesus. Not only did Frank want him to kiss up to the three holdouts on the board, he wanted Matt to use Frank's script to do so. The only good that had come of that little meeting with him earlier was finding out that the board meeting had been moved up two hours.

What it had also done was remind him that he hadn't thought about the board, or London, in days. He'd been too busy thinking about Sam.

For the first time since the carrot of running the London office had been dangled in front of him, Matt wasn't feeling entirely positive about the job. The idea of putting the Atlantic Ocean between him and Sam made him uncomfortable. It was crazy. They'd seen each other a few times over the course of the past week. Not nearly often enough for him to have any thoughts that would impact his career.

He'd probably wake up tomorrow and be back to his old self. The London office was his, and while he wouldn't grovel to get it, he had gone to some extreme lengths to win the prize. He'd wanted it so badly.

"Where's your girl?"

His father joined him in this out-of-the-way spot.

"In the ladies' room."

"Your mother is very pleased with the fund-raising tonight. I know she'd like to brag about it to you. And it looks as if Bannister and Lee are coming around to your side of the fence. Now that they've had time to digest the Tokyo hotel deal, they're seeing you in a different light."

"I've done deals like this before."

"That's part of it. You've consistently done good work, Matthew, and it's being noticed. Oh, and your sister is upset you haven't brought your girlfriend to meet her."

"She's not—"

"Speaking of which," his father continued, "bringing Ms. O'Connel to the party was a very clever move. Choosing brains over beauty for once? Well played. I think you impressed a lot of people here tonight. They're finally acknowledging that you're invested in building the company, not just waiting to get your trust fund."

Matt stared at his father. "That's what you think?"

"About the trust fund?"

"About why I brought Sam." Matt took a quick look around to make sure she wasn't within hearing range. "Politics had nothing to do with me bringing her here tonight, but just hearing that makes me wish I hadn't."

"Don't be a fool, Matthew. Whether you meant it isn't as important as how it was perceived."

Just as Matt was about to slam a hole straight through that theory, his father smiled at someone behind Matt's shoulder. He knew without looking that it was Sam.

"I was hoping you'd return before I had to go," Charles said. "Matthew's mother and sister would love to see you again."

Before Sam could utter a word, Matt took her hand in his. "Sorry. We'll catch them another time. We're leaving."

"So soon?" His father looked stunned, then angry. "We haven't had the finale yet. There's still the cake and the annual fund-raising report."

"Sorry. I'm sure everyone will forgive my absence this one year. I'll see you on Monday."

"Matthew."

He started walking away, Sam following at his side, but then Matt remembered something. "One sec." He turned back to his father, pulling Sam's check out of his pocket. "Give this to Mom, would you? I'm sure she'll be a lot more forgiving once she sees it."

The orchestra started playing an old Beatles song, drowning out most of the noise in the room, but Matt could have sworn he heard his father sputtering. It didn't matter. Matt was mad enough to spit, but he didn't for a second regret bringing Sam. People should have looked at him enviously, but not for the wrong reasons.

Hell, there wasn't a woman at the gala who could hold a candle to Sam.

SAM CLOSED HER eyes and let her head drop back as Matt loosened her skirt and let it sink to her ankles. He'd taken such care with her belt and peplum top.

Now she was wearing just her heels and her tiny panties in the middle of his bedroom at the apartment.

Closing her eyes had been an attempt at letting everything fall away except this moment.

But she couldn't release the sound of Matt's father's words. How clever Matt had been to bring her. Choosing brains over beauty.

It hurt on so many levels.

She hated to think Matt had ulterior motives in inviting her to the gala. But the fact that he'd asked her at all was odd. So, if it was politically motivated, did that negate the wonderful experience?

No. Of course not. Why shouldn't he have made some political headway with her? It would have been fine *if* he'd told her. But he hadn't, and she wished now that she'd heard more of the conversation instead of doing a lap back to the restroom before joining them.

"Sammy? You okay?"

Matt's voice broke through her unsettling thoughts. When she opened her eyes, the star-filled galaxy above her head soothed her.

"I'm fine," she said, trying to make it true. "Just letting everything wash over me."

"I'd like to help with that, if you'll just step away from that poofy skirt."

"It's not poof. It's chiffon."

He gave her a look. "As if you knew that before this afternoon."

She smiled, and that was genuine. But she still needed a moment. "I'll be happy to step away, but before we get this rolling, could you please bring us some water? I think I had too much champagne. I'm going to get some aspirin. I hate waking up with a headache."

"I should have thought of that," he said. "Although leaving you isn't easy." With a quick dart of a kiss, he went to the door, already stripped down to his black boxer briefs.

Her view was outstanding.

Sadly, as soon as he was gone from her sight, her stupid brain spilled a big mess inside her. Everything had been so perfect. She'd let herself believe his invitation to the ball had been romantic.

Oh, God. She wasn't just walking toward a heartbreak; she was already there.

It was supposed to have been a fling. At twenty-nine, she should have known better. Yes, a person couldn't help whom he or she loved, but a person could also walk away before that love had a chance to blossom. For all she knew, tonight might be her last with him. The gala was over, and tomorrow he was most likely going to go stay at the hotel because the board meeting was on Monday. And by Monday night, he would have used up his reasons to stay in Boston. Matt traveled extensively. His home base was New York, but his office was the world.

Regardless of whether or not this was their last night together, she was going to make sure it was the best night she'd ever had. There was no reason for her to worry about falling for him. That die had been cast. Yes, she would have a hard time getting over him, and life would be miserable for a while. But he was here now. She had him tonight. She might as well get the most out of it.

Love him as if he loved her back.

It took barely a minute to retrieve the aspirin from

the bathroom, and when she returned to the bedroom, Matt was already there with a couple of water bottles and a bowl of red grapes. The way he looked at her, as if he wanted to remember every last little thing about her, made her shivery inside. He looked hungry for her. Starved. And his briefs didn't do anything to hide his thickening cock.

"I can't decide if I want to strip those panties off with my teeth or keep them on and do wicked things to them."

She wiggled her butt a bit, knowing her blush was painting her pink from her chest up. "You know, in those tight black briefs, you look like a superhero. Not the Hulk. More like Captain America or Thor."

"Stop. I've already got a swelled head from having you as my date tonight. Besides, I've made my decision about your panties."

She sighed, determined to take the compliment at face value and excited to see what would come next. "Show me."

He was nude before she finished the last word and headed toward her. His steps were slow and his gaze calculating. She felt pinned to the spot. Everything about him screamed a delicious kind of danger.

When he got to her, he moved in close enough for her to feel his heat. His hand went to the back of her head, then into her hair, as they met in a kiss. Their bodies weren't touching yet. Just their lips and her head in his hand, and when his tongue thrust into her mouth, she forgot about the hand.

God. She'd miss his kisses. Deep and intense, they left little time for breathing. It felt as if she was being claimed. And when he pressed against her, his free hand on the small of her back, she felt that amazing connection of theirs. Sam held on, dizzy and weak in the knees.

His cock eventually pressed against her tummy. He maneuvered them to the bed, where they pushed the covers down and found their pillows. Finally, she was in his arms.

"You take my breath away," he said. "With your Rita Hayworth hair, and knowing you were braless under that gown… Jesus, you almost did me in."

"You weren't so bad yourself."

"Stay tonight," hc said.

She tensed. Of course he must have felt it. The way his smile dimmed made her want to change her mind. "We'll see," she said. Then she kissed him. Hard.

When it was breathe or die, she gasped and leaned over to the bedside table to grab a condom. Then she took hold of his erection. It was his turn to gasp. "You're very, very hard," she said.

"That's your fault."

"You want me to…?" She stroked him. "I have these painted nails. They look pretty nice when I do this."

Matt groaned. "Just imagining that makes me want to come. So wait. Better stop, okay?"

She sighed dramatically but let him go. Only to tease him mercilessly while putting the condom on.

Quick as a wink, he was between her thighs, bracing himself above her. "I want you. So much. I'm going to miss this like crazy."

Looking away, she clamped her eyes shut, willing the lump in her throat to go away. Before he could call her out, she reached between them to guide him, her legs loosely around his waist.

"Sam? Wait a second. Oh, damn."

She'd rubbed the head of his cock against her wet heat.

His groan was deep and rough, and it was easy enough to get him centered.

He pushed in. But not fast, as she'd expected. With gentle fingers, he urged her to look at him again.

When he gazed into her eyes, it was as deep a bond as she'd ever felt. As if they'd stripped away everything else in the whole world, leaving the two of them raw and naked.

"I didn't expect this," he whispered.

"Expect what?"

"You."

"I'm still just Sam."

"Oh, no," he said, moving a bit now. Plunging deeper. "You're so much more. I'm fascinated by you, Samantha O'Connel. The way you think, the sound of your laughter. Your obsession with everything vintage while you're on the cutting edge of tech. The way you stood up for me tonight. I wasn't kidding when I said you were terrific. I was proud, and glad, and I ached to be right here."

Her nails, silver and sparkly, dug into his back, making him raise his head and hiss.

"Jesus."

"You," she said, pressing her thighs against him, preparing for his next move, "made every…" She lost the sentence. It was a compliment, but she'd have to tell him later.

"I made every what?"

She shook her head and raised her hips to meet his thrust. "You were awesome."

"No, you were—" Cut short by his own groan, he was pumping now, pulling almost all the way out, then driving back in again like a steam engine. As if he wasn't in control of his own movements.

Her hips were held up by a miracle, but she was so tight that every time he drove into her, her throbbing clit got a full dose of bliss. Shivers raced up and down her spine and she was hanging on for dear life. "Kiss me now, damn you."

He did. He kissed her until they were both crying out in each other's mouths. He hit the magic button and she came. So hard that she almost knocked him over. But he held his position like a trooper. A desperate trooper who looked as if he was in exquisite pain, and then he froze.

But even after the moans quieted and the shuddering stopped, he didn't pull out. He left his still-hard penis in her, and as he helped her back down to the mattress, he pulsed inside her. He looked at her with no wicked grin, no smart-ass response. His forehead was dotted with a sheen of sweat and his arms trembled as he watched her. "I don't want to stop," he whispered.

She squeezed him, unable to ease off even when she saw him wince. But she couldn't help it.

They hadn't just had sex, or screwed, or whatever. They'd made love.

Incredible. Intimate. Love.

Oh, she was in deep, deep trouble.

13

THE WAY SAM FIT, tucked against his side, filled Matt with a peace he hadn't experienced before. He was wiped out. From the party, from his father, his uncles. From the incredible lovemaking with Sam that made everything else fade into the background.

She smelled like sex and jasmine. The walls were dark but for the fireflies and the stars shining above him. It was a moment he'd remember for a very long time.

"I don't want to move," she said, a little breathless.

"Good. I don't want you to move."

"But I have to go to the bathroom."

He kissed her temple. "Why didn't you go when I did?"

"Foolish. Lazy. Take your pick."

"Okay, well, here's a plus. When you come back, we can spoon."

No response. So she'd picked up on his hint that she should spend the night. He kept his breathing easy, tried hard not to hold her any tighter.

"That is a plus," she said so softly that he barely heard her.

He couldn't stop his smile. Didn't want to, now that he thought about it. "Good." He loosened the arm he had wrapped around her and she rolled to the side before she stood. He stared at her in wonder. That hair of hers. Would he ever stop being fascinated by it? He'd bet most people thought it was from a bottle, but he knew it was the real deal. It felt like silk in his hands. While she was in the bathroom, he did some rearranging— put the pillows back on the bed, picked up the blankets from the floor. He even ate a few grapes before he got under the covers.

Hands clasped behind his head, he waited, watching the walls transform themselves all around him. To be this creative, Sam had to have a romantic streak in her, even if she wouldn't admit it. Then he noticed something odd. A red light high up on the wall to his left. She'd told him about the sensors, but this looked like a camera. No, Sam would never.

When she came back, she dropped her robe by the end of the bed and looked at him. "What's wrong?" she asked.

"Is that a camera?"

She climbed in beside him. "What? Where?"

He pulled her close with one hand and pointed with the other. "There."

"That's not supposed to be on. Not when there are any heat signatures in the apartment.

"Monitor 4G," she said. "Admin number 4857828. Camera 3 maintenance, main bedroom, playback."

A monitor appeared on the wall. Right away he saw thermal images of the two of them. They were kissing. And stripping. He had to admit it was kind of sexy. He looked over at Sam. "You're blushing."

"Great. So wonderful to know I'm caught on every frequency— Hold on. What's this?"

The thermal image was replaced by a standard view. Of them. Naked. And kissing, and them falling onto the bed, pushing everything down. Sam gasped and covered her mouth. "So how do you turn that off?" Matt asked.

"Why?"

He turned his attention back to her, expecting her to burst into flames at any second. But she'd lowered her hand and the blush was already fading. "Because we've just made a sex tape," he said.

"I know."

"Sam."

It seemed she couldn't tear her gaze away from the wall. "What?" She finally spared him a quick glance. "Aren't you curious? I have no idea what went wrong, although I've had some issues with the programming in the past. It might stop or go back to thermal. Then again, it might not."

"You want to watch us?" He sat forward, leaning on his elbows. "Really?"

"I don't know." She gave a small shrug. "Do you?"

"Is that a trick question?"

She laughed, but he sensed the nervousness behind it. "I'm going to destroy it, of course, but before I do— I mean, why not? It's just us."

"It's one angle, and that's not going to change. It's focused on the whole bed. Are you sure you're ready for that?"

She grinned and nodded.

"Jesus, you're full of surprises, aren't you?"

Her expression fell. "Look, we don't have to watch it. I just thought—"

"I want to." He caught her arm when she started to get up. "I'm sorry—I just don't want you to become uncomfortable."

She pulled him down into a quick kiss. "If either one of us says stop, we'll stop it. Okay?"

"Okay," he said, not sure if this was a mistake or not. He was tempted to skip watching the tape and just watch her.

She perched on her knees, running her hand over Matt's chest as she watched. "This is weird. Do I really look that pale? And awkward?"

"What the hell are you talking about? You have porcelain skin, the softest I've ever touched. As for awkward, oh, honey, you are no such thing."

"But look," she said, pointing at where her legs were akimbo and her hair was half in her face.

"All I see is a beautiful woman. Nothing about you taking pleasure from your body is awkward."

"You're prejudiced."

"Yep."

They were quiet for a moment. Watching. It wasn't the kind of sex you'd see in porn. It was slow. No music. But it was raw and exciting. The feeling of being inside her swept over him, making his cock harden, which was quite a feat, and his belly tense. It was a little crazy, considering what he'd just figured out. He touched her cheek, wondering if she was seeing the same thing he was. They weren't just having sex. They were making love.

By all rights the realization should've scared the hell out of him.

"This makes me want you all over again," he whispered.

"Prove it," she said, her voice huskier than normal.

She lifted herself up, turned around and straddled his thighs. After studying him for a moment, she smiled. "I think there's a way we can both watch the tape and do a live re-creation. If you're up to it, that is."

All his blood rushed south, but he was still able to nod.

A TICKLE WOKE Matt from the best dream he'd had in a long time. When he swiped the offending source of that tickle, he remembered. An even better reality was in his arms, her hair wandering over from what had become their pillow.

He'd imagined waking up to a note, with only the cold dent in the pillow to remind him of the night they'd shared. But he'd finally got his wish: he would get to spend a morning with Sam. They'd have some great coffee, take a shower together, and with any luck—

"What?" Sam turned and nearly beaned him with her head as she sat up. "Oh."

"Good morning to you, too."

She blinked at him, last night's makeup giving her adorable raccoon eyes. "Sorry," she said, trying to hold back a yawn, then giving it up. It was a very big yawn that made him yawn in return. "Did I wake you?"

"I think I woke you, even though I'm not sure how." He turned on his back and checked the light behind the shades. It looked weirdly bright. "What time is it?"

"Oh, my God." Sam let out a soft squeak. "It's almost eleven."

"Seriously? I never sleep this late." He braced himself, expecting her to shoot out of bed.

But she didn't. "Me neither." She lay down again, on her side, her gaze meandering down his body as she rested her hand over his.

"Thank you," he whispered.

"For what?"

"Spending the night. I liked waking up with you."

Her lashes came down. "I've never done this before. Slept all night with someone."

"Ever?"

"Nope."

He turned his hand up and threaded their fingers. "Well, I'm glad to be the first."

"It's not as if I've been with many guys. So you might be the first and last."

Matt had no idea what to say to that. Something about how she should make more time in her life for dating? That he wanted to be the one and only?

Did he want that?

"I don't recall sleeping till eleven, either," she said. "Well, obviously I must have when I was very young."

"Sleeping late stopped for me my first year of law school," Matt said. "Since then I've always had work to do. Even when I want to sleep in, my body is on a strict schedule. Makes hopping time zones a pain in the ass."

Sam squeezed his hand but didn't say anything, although it looked as if she might.

"What is it, Sammy?"

She kept her lashes lowered. "I was just wondering how much longer you planned on being here."

Matt held back a grimace at the sickening thought that she'd overheard something about London last night. It wasn't as if it were precisely a secret. But the fact remained—he hadn't mentioned the possibility of his moving.

"Not that I'm trying to get rid of you." She was looking at him now, but the little crinkle above her nose told him his answer mattered. "It's just that Clark might have booked someone to come stay here next week. And since the gala is over and your, um, board meeting is tomorrow…" Her hand slipped away and she grabbed the covers that had fallen to her waist and pulled them up to her chin. "You've probably already booked your flight to New York, so I was just…wondering."

Ah. This wasn't about London.

His relief lasted all of five seconds.

It was still possible she did want to get rid of him. She was behind with work and he'd been a big distraction, so he couldn't blame her if she did. Jesus. It had been her hesitation that made him nervous. She wasn't normally like that. Sam just said whatever was on her mind.

This must be Sam at her most vulnerable. She'd been more relaxed at the damn gala. A few more seconds and the cloud lifted from his sleep-deprived brain. The question wasn't about logistics or the apartment; it was more personal. Sam wanted to know about *them*.

"Don't mind me," she said. "I'm just rambling. I mean, this is why Clark handles the business side of things. You don't have to leave unless you want to. It doesn't matter, and I should get up because it's eleven and…"

He kissed her, then moved back a little. "I'll probably be in Boston through the week, but if you or Clark has booked the apartment, I can always stay at the hotel."

"No," she said, and there was the happy Sam in her voice again. "No, seriously. Stay as long as you like."

Now he was really worried. There wasn't a way this thing wouldn't end with them apart. He'd probably be in London, and she'd be in her lab, too busy to get away for a day, let alone a couple of weeks. They'd both be up to their ears in work. But he wasn't about to bring that up now. Not until he knew for sure if he had the London job.

"So are we staying in or going out for breakfast? We can get dim sum at Myers & Chang," he said. "Unless you have to work."

"Nope. I'm not going anywhere near the lab today."

A few days ago he would've been sending up fireworks that she was willing to spend all this time with him. Now he was wondering if he'd done her a huge disservice.

Hell, he'd worry later, he thought as she snuggled closer.

For now, he kissed her. Until her stomach grumbled so loudly they both cracked up.

"THERE'S EVERYTHING WE need to make waffles," Sam said. "I specifically made sure of that."

"I have no objection to waffles," Matt said, amused by the argument they were having. "I'm just saying eggs and bacon would make a nice addition to the menu."

"But I like my waffles a lot."

"And…?"

"Notice I said *waffles*."

"Ah, so no room at the inn, eh?"

She walked between his legs, which wasn't difficult, because he was sitting on the counter that faced the living room. "Exactly," she said. "Although what you said about bacon has a certain…"

"Je ne sais quoi?"

"I was going to say *salty flavor*, but *je ne sais quoi* works, too. Dammit."

He wondered what she was cursing about until he

recognized her ringtone coming from the purse she'd put on the couch.

"I should get that." He watched her go. Damn, she looked good wearing his T-shirt and boxers.

"Yeah, what's up?" she said.

As she listened, he could see her good mood dissolve like Alka-Seltzer in water. It had to be Clark. No one could douse her mood like him. At least, from what Matt had observed. For all he knew, Clark farted rainbows when he had Sam all to himself.

"What, so he can't wait a few extra days? Screw him." Now she was pacing. Matt deflated. He had the distinct feeling their breakfast was going to be a nonstarter. But what made him really uneasy was thinking about their earlier conversation. While he was jetting off to his job, he'd be leaving her with a shitload of work to do. Well, hell. He might not see a solution to their work conundrum, but at least Sam was going to get a damn waffle.

As he took out the waffle maker and the ingredients, he listened to Sam.

"I know we have a contract, Clark. What I'm saying is that even people with a contract can take a few days off. I told you he wanted it too soon to begin with."

Matt paused between cracking two eggs. That didn't sound like—

"Ugh, fine. You said that. Who cares? It was true."

Matt nodded to himself and cracked the second egg.

"No, I don't want to get sued. Come on. Offer something constructive instead of just being a butthead."

Matt smiled as he measured flour and poured oil into the bowl.

"Oh, nice. So now it's threats? You're not farming out

my work to Tina. She's got a project, and she isn't familiar with the job."

Matt got out the whisk, but before he put it in the bowl, he turned, trying to get Sam's attention. He wasn't very subtle about it, waving the whisk in the air.

"Hold on. I— Hold on." She pressed a button on her phone. "Yes?"

Her voice was a little sharp, which he understood. "If you need to go to the lab, that's fine. I've actually got a few hours' worth of work to do before the board meeting tomorrow. We can meet up later."

"I don't know. We were going to have breakfast and—"

"We'll still have breakfast. Then I was planning to kick you out anyway, so you might as well go into work."

She just looked at him.

He knew she could see through part of his lie. They'd already talked about spending the day together. But he could've just remembered he had something to do before the board meeting. He didn't, but this way, she wouldn't feel guilty.

"Fine." She pressed another button on her phone. "I'll be there in an hour."

Matt started whisking the batter, satisfied he'd done the right thing, even though it felt like hell to give up a whole day alone with Sam. He'd wanted that. Badly.

The light had turned green on the waffle iron, so he poured the first batch. It was an odd machine. Much thinner than the kind that made the Belgian waffles he was used to. But it looked foolproof.

He glanced at her again. "Why don't you go change while this is cooking?"

She looked sad but nodded.

"I'll have your waffles and coffee waiting for you,"

he said, keeping his tone light when all he wanted to do was throw everything at the wall.

She smiled. Took his face between her hands and kissed him soundly.

He put an arm around her. A mistake, for sure. Because now he didn't want to let her go. But he did and then watched her hurry from the room.

The food was ready by the time she returned. From the damp ends of her hair, he could tell she'd taken a very short shower. Dammit, he'd wanted to take a long one with her.

She took a stick of butter, the maple syrup and the whole plateful of waffles to the counter by the stools.

"Huh." He'd planned on sharing, but he guessed he'd have to make his own.

"This is delicious," she said through her mouthful. "Better than the mix in the pantry."

Well, shit. "There was a mix?"

AN HOUR LATER Matt was watching a movie on HBO when his dad called. "Hey, Dad."

"Good afternoon, Matthew."

"You sound cheerful."

"Do I? Well, that must be because it looks as if we've got a lock on that London job of yours. Truit is still a holdout, but we don't need that old windbag anyway. I don't expect any surprises, but I won't say congratulations yet."

Matt should have been on his feet doing a fist pump, excited as hell. "That's fantastic, Dad. How'd you get Bannister and Lee on board?"

His father went into all the details, and Matt had to force himself to pay attention. It wasn't meant to feel like this. All the effort, the planning, the hours spent. Now taking over the London office had lost its luster. No, that wasn't exactly true. He welcomed the challenge. Or would have if it didn't put this thing between him and Sam into the dead file.

"What? No, I'm excited. I am. I just don't want to go overboard until the votes are in, that's all."

His father agreed that was smart. They talked a few more minutes and then said their goodbyes.

The movie was no longer of interest to Matt, and sitting there with nothing to do but think was out of the question. He paced to the window, smiling as the floor tiles lit up with each footfall. Sam had an amazing imagination. No wonder she was slammed with orders. And as far as he knew, the apartment's innovations weren't actually on the market yet.

Goddammit. He ran his hands over his face. Was he ever going to be able to stop thinking about her? The mess he'd created was growing by leaps and bounds inside his head. Sticking around would just make him crazy.

There was only one thing he could do right now that might help. For a split second he experienced a prick of fear that he was reverting to his old destructive habits. But no, this was about needing some release. A workout was better than downing half a bottle of scotch.

Carrick was at the Southie gym when Matt showed up. But since it was a Sunday, there were fewer boxers around. He'd make do with the bags, but that wasn't what he wanted.

"What are you doing here, son?" Matt noticed the older man was walking with a slight limp. He'd missed that last week.

"Looking for some ring time."

"I might be able to fit you in. Hank," he called out, "put Matt's name on the big board, will ya? See who wants in."

Someone from the benches on the other side of the ring called out, "Hey, pretty boy. We still got to be careful around your ugly mug?"

It was tempting to throw caution to the wind and just go for broke, but he still had to meet with the board. "Yep, watch the face. But everything else is fair game."

He didn't care about the taunting. While it should have felt good to realize he wasn't a completely reckless kid anymore, all it did was make him feel...sad.

14

HER CELL PHONE RANG. It was Matt. Foolish of her to give him his own ringtone when he'd be gone soon.

Not a good thing to think about now.

She checked the time. Damn, she was already ten minutes late meeting him. "Hey."

"Hi. Listen, I'm heading your way. Should be there in under five minutes. Sorry."

"Don't apologize. I'm going to be even later. Anyway, I didn't mean for us to meet here. I meant the apartment. But I'm not done my work, and there's no way to put it off."

"Oh," Matt said, his voice dipping.

She knew she shouldn't feel so pleased that she'd disappointed him, but it was reassuring. "I'm probably going to be another hour. I can't imagine it taking much longer than that."

"Tell you what. Since I'm already close, why don't I come by the lab? I can amuse myself while you work. I promise not to bother you."

Clark would freak out. There was no way. "I'll go

you one better," she said. "You know my house is behind the lab, right?"

"Yeah."

"I'll have Tina dash over there and turn off the alarm
system and leave it unlocked. It's still a mess, but it's
more comfortable than here. I've got a lot of stuff to play
with. You'll have a good time."

"The only thing I want to play with is you."

Sam pressed her lips together. "Stop it," she said, glancing around as if someone could've heard him. "And don't
be afraid to touch the games. I break things regularly.
Okay?"

"Okay."

"Oh, wait. If you do break something? Write down
what you did, okay? I want to see if I can duplicate it,
then create a fix."

"You're such a geek."

She grinned for the first time since she'd left him that
morning. "I know."

After she put her cell phone back at the edge of her
work space, she felt Clark's censure without having to
look. He'd been grumpy all day. She couldn't complain
about it. This was taking up his Sunday, too.

And Coulson, the prick, had been completely irratio-
nal about moving the deadline. Goddamn newbie. She
was doing him a favor by even taking the contract. In
her field, compromises were part of the landscape. There
were too many unknowns to commit to anything hard
and fast. It should have been a piece of cake. The upstairs crew were handling most of it on their own. But
there'd been a problem with the power source that only
Sam could fix.

She was almost there. In fact, with a few more adjustments, she'd be able to run the 3-D simulation and make sure everything worked as planned.

Then she'd get to see Matt. Though any time she got with him was now bittersweet, it was still more exciting than anything else in her life. Because it had an expiration date? Maybe. That was a better theory than the other—that she was completely, hopelessly in love.

MATT HAD A bruise on his chin that he hadn't had that morning. It begged a lot of questions. Sam would ask, but she didn't wake him. Not yet.

She'd been later than she'd hoped, so it wasn't a surprise he'd crashed. She liked watching him sleep, just as she had all those years ago on her sixteenth birthday. He looked comfortable on her ugly old couch. Friends had hinted that she might want to think about getting a sofa that didn't look like something she'd found in a back alley. It was years out of date, but she didn't care. The leather was worn in just the right places and it was perfect for watching TV or gaming. As if she had the time to do either.

"Hey," he said, in a croak that made something tug in her chest.

"Hey. Sorry I was late."

"It's okay. It stinks that you had to work." He sat up and ran a hand through his hair. But he hissed in a breath at the move and winced for a good two seconds.

"What happened?" she asked.

"What?"

Sam pushed back the coffee table to give her room so she could sit down in front of him. "That bruise on your chin. The way you're moving. Were you in an accident?"

"No."

"What, then?"

"I was working out. At a gym."

"Did you get into a fight over a machine or something?"

Matt chuckled. "I was sparring."

"You mean how boxers spar?" Sam was almost afraid to touch him. "Because I don't think you're supposed to get hurt sparring."

"It's not so bad. You should see the other guy."

"That isn't funny."

"No, I'm serious. Juan looks a lot worse than me." He laughed, but the wince came back and he touched his ribs.

Sam reached over, lifted his blue henley and saw another couple of bruises right where he'd touched. "What the hell, Matt?"

"Look, I can explain."

"Yeah, well, do that, please, while I get you some ice. Since when do you box?"

"It's a great workout, I swear. I've been doing it since college."

She pulled out a bag of frozen peas and two bottles of beer from the fridge. "I remember you occasionally had bruises, but you always gave excuses for them. I just thought you were clumsy. Why didn't you say?"

He applied the peas. "I didn't want you guys to know." With his free hand, he took a swig of beer. "It was a great way to get rid of pent-up energy. Punching the bag, then punching a sparring partner. I got into some mixed martial arts, too, and then, senior year, I did a little street fighting but quit fast. Too brutal for me. And my grades started slipping."

"Logan and Rick didn't know?"

"Logan figured it out. Gave me a hell of a lecture. But I never understood why. It's a completely legit sport. Boxing, not the street fighting. Hell, he was into martial arts himself and going to the firing range... It doesn't matter. It's a sport, that's all. This afternoon I went to my old gym. Just to say hi to the guys."

"That's some 'hi.'" She looked pointedly at his chin.

"Complete accident. The helmet slipped."

"What happened to your ribs?" she asked. "Did your parents know?"

"Jesus. No. Not then and not now."

Sam wondered why he hadn't been at the apartment working, as he'd said he'd be, but she didn't want to ask. "I don't have to worry about you, do I?"

"Yeah, but not about the boxing," he said, his voice taking on a mischievous tone. "What you should be concerned about is the fact that we haven't kissed once since you got home."

He leaned forward and she met him halfway, welcoming the feel of his lips on hers, his woodsy scent. But he pulled away too quickly for her liking.

"Come over here with me." He patted a spot on the couch. "I love your place, by the way. It's totally you. The mantel with your action figures. Wonder Woman, Supergirl, Hermione Granger... Jean Grey from *X-Men*? I didn't know they had one for her."

"They didn't. I had it made for me. But now that I have a 3-D printer, I can make my own."

"Excellent," he said. "Also? This couch is supercomfortable."

"Exactly," she said, more emphatically than necessary. "Wait right there. I'll be back in a sec. And points to you for knowing who everyone was on the mantel."

Sam hurried to her bathroom, where she found a big Ace wrap and a tube of arnica gel. He smiled at her return, causing a tingle to skitter all the way down her body.

It felt both odd and intimate to be patching him up. Rubbing the ointment over his taut skin, then wrapping his chest, despite his protests.

"I look ridiculous."

"You deserve it. Boxing. I'll never understand it."

"It helps me let off steam." He gripped her chin in his hand and pulled her into the first really good kiss since their morning had been interrupted. He teased her lower lip with the edge of his top teeth, then traced over the same part with his tongue. When Sam thought of all the men who'd kissed her, and there weren't that many, Matt was in a class by himself. He made her nipples hard without even touching them, her thighs squeeze together with the flick of his tongue against hers. When her hand ventured up his thigh, she let him know it wasn't a one-way dialogue.

When they came up for air, Matt was breathing hard and smiling. "I'm so glad you're home." He grabbed his beer and leaned back, bringing her with him.

"Wait," she said when something poked her in the butt. "What's...?" Sam found a picture frame that had been wedged behind the sofa cushion. "This is us."

"I found it on your mantel, too. Jesus, we were young."

"I was fifteen when this was taken." She smiled at the images of Logan and Rick. "And you guys. Wow. I continue to be amazed that three such astonishingly hot guys were my protectors." She paused, thinking for a moment. "Except back then I was such a geek I didn't know Logan and Rick were hot. But don't tell them that."

"You didn't mention me. Does that mean…?" Matt's eyebrows were raised and he was grinning.

"Shut up." She smiled and studied the picture, thinking about what Kensey had shared with her about Matt covering the rent. Sam wished so much that she could thank him but she'd given her word. "You really were the best thing that could have happened to me back then. And after, when you took off to become a lawyer, Clark swooped in and he was just as kind."

Matt took the picture from her and studied it, his smile melting into something else entirely. "I owe you a long-overdue apology."

"For not telling me about the boxing?"

"No," he said, meeting her gaze. "For the night you turned sixteen."

Heat spread through her like a wildfire. Of course she knew exactly what he was talking about. She could still see him so clearly, standing at her bedroom door, his hair rumpled, a lock falling across his forehead.

He'd been at a party that night but rushed back to the dorm just past midnight. She'd been working late, unaware of the time. He told her he wanted to be the first to kiss her happy birthday. As if there would be a line.

That night had been monumental to her. She'd already had a crush on him, but when he kissed her, she was a goner. She knew he'd simply intended to give her an innocent peck on the lips. But it hadn't ended there. And it was all her doing. She'd pressed closer. Probably the bravest thing she'd ever done until that point. She could smell the alcohol on his breath, but it hadn't bothered her. Before then, she'd hated the scent of beer, but she'd grown to love it over the years, starting with that night.

The kiss had gone on a little bit longer, but when she'd parted her lips, he'd pulled away.

"I should never have gone to see you when I was drunk," he said.

"It was sweet. I had such a massive crush on you."

"I know."

"What? How did you know?"

"You'd just turned sixteen. You weren't yet versed in the game. You were brilliant and also transparent. That's what made what I did inexcusable. I didn't realize I was being a tease. I let the alcohol take over whatever sense I had."

"But I wanted it. I was thrilled you'd kissed me."

"Thrilled? When I pulled back, you immediately thought you'd done something wrong. You begged me to try again, to teach you how to kiss me the way you should. You were so convinced you'd screwed things up, when you'd done nothing wrong. I felt like such a shit."

Sam shook her head, not remembering any part of what he'd described. "Are you sure this is me you're talking about? I didn't do any of that." Her heart was thumping so hard she wondered if he could hear it. "Like you said, you were drunk. Maybe you don't remember correctly."

"I wish…" He hung his head. "Evidently, being a prick sobered me up some. So sorry, Sammy. I think you might've rewritten some of that night. I can't say I blame you. Then I made everything worse by falling asleep on your bed. Probably snored up a storm. And dammit, you were just a kid. I had no business being in your room at all."

"I'll have to trust that you're telling me the truth about what I did."

"You don't recall me holding your hand while I sat next to you?"

She nodded. He'd been so sweet. He'd told her she was young but he liked her anyway.

"I told you that it was wrong that I'd kissed you. That you were too young, and then I asked you not to tell anyone. I made you promise to keep it from Logan and Rick. Do you remember that part?"

"Perfectly," she said. His recollection of that night's events surprised her. She'd never felt resentful, and she didn't now. Maybe a little sad that he'd spoiled her memories. She smiled, wanting him to believe that she didn't hold him responsible for anything, even what happened afterward. "I must have blocked most of it out. All my recollections of that night have been ridiculously happy."

"Maybe, but you remember something else, don't you?" He watched her closely, waiting, the regret in his eyes painful for her to see.

"It's nothing. It's just—when you begged me to keep it a secret, I thought it was because you were ashamed of being with me. After that you hardly talked to me—"

"Oh, sweetheart," he said, taking her hand. "I was ashamed of myself, not you. And I didn't want to get my ass kicked by Logan and Rick."

"I can see that now." She smiled and squeezed his hand. "Oh, my God, is that why you took up boxing? In case Logan and—"

With a laugh, Matt brought her hand up for a quick kiss. "No, I'd already been going to the gym by then. But I admit I purposely kept my distance from you after that." He looked into her eyes with a sincerity that brought a lump to her throat. "I hope I haven't opened old wounds by filling in the blanks for you. I'm not sure I would've said anything if I had known that you remembered the night so fondly, but I'm sorry for that, too. Please forgive me, Sam."

"Oh, Matt." She leaned in and kissed him hard. "Of course I do. In fact, you apologized to me that night."

He stroked her cheek. "Well, I'm glad that I somehow managed to find you again, now that we're both older and wiser…"

"Wiser? You?"

"Hey," he said, pulling her closer.

"Your hobby is punching and being punched."

"First of all, I don't have the time anymore. And second, there's more to it than—"

"I've seen the movies. No explanation is going to change my mind. Anyway, I don't need to agree with everything you do to like you." Or to be in love with him, she thought, but she would never tell him that.

"And the reverse is also true, though I haven't found anything I don't like about you yet." He leaned back and looked at her through squinted eyes. "You were captivating at the gala. Whether people knew who you were or not. I think you've overcome your social anxiety, Sam."

Sam rose and hoped her dismissive wave was enough to distract him. They had so little time left. It might ruin things if he knew that just looking at him gave her the same thrill as it had all those years ago. There were no two ways about it: she wanted this man. His friendship, his touch, his advice, his kindness.

This was what love felt like. All the little things just fell into place. And as always, she was navigating this crazy new world of emotions alone.

She knew they could never be together. She might have been useful on his arm for a night, but for the long run? They might as well live in different universes. Just knowing what his family thought about her would make it impossible for them to be together if he weren't consumed with his job and she weren't consumed by hers.

"Wait. Where are you going?" he asked. "We haven't planned out our night yet."

She stopped halfway to the kitchen. "Right," she said, although they both knew where they'd eventually end up. "You have a choice, Wilkinson. *Buffy* marathon or 'House of the Dead 2.'"

"No way. You've still got 'House of the Dead 2'? My God, woman. You're a hoarder. That game came out in, what—"

"In 1998."

"Hoarder! What would I find if I opened any of these other doors?"

"Depends. If you're lucky and don't cry like a toddler when I kick your ass, you might find my bedroom behind one of them."

He was on his feet, frantically trying to unwrap his bandage. "First of all, I get a handicap."

"Why? Because you have a little bruise?"

"Ha. Funny."

"Why, then?" She folded her arms, watching him fight the bandage. "We both know the game."

"You own the fucker. It's been like eight years since I played it."

"What, you think I have time to play? And it's a damn two-player game. You know I don't like to play those solo."

"Fine. No handicap. And for the record, my ass isn't the one that's going to be kicked."

Sam giggled. She couldn't help it. This was ridiculous,

but she couldn't wait to play him again. "You stay there. I'll get the Wii. And the Perfect Shots. Oh, and dibs on being James Taylor."

"Not fair." Even Matt couldn't deny he'd just sounded as if he were twelve. "God, you're already cheating. You know I wanted to be him. I'm always James Taylor."

"Yeah, well, *Gary*, I suppose you're just going to have to suck it up."

He caught her by the waist and pulled her into his arms. He kissed her hard. "You know what I think?"

"I'm afraid to ask. Who knows what goes on in that head of yours?"

He gave her the half smile she liked so much. "I think we should have an appetizer first," he said and bit her earlobe.

She shivered in agreement.

"Load, you idiot, load!"

Matt turned the gun away from the game, seconds away from dying a horrible death at the hands of an ax-wielding headless killing puppet. His gun reloaded, he fired at the screen furiously until Kuarl was dead as a doornail. "Got 'im!"

"Too bad you're going to be killed by Zeal, sucker!"

"Dammit, why didn't you—"

"We're playing against each other. What am I supposed to do? Hold your hand?"

The insult didn't sting as much since he got to watch Sam slam her way through the Venetian labyrinth, killing zombies as if that were what she was born to do. There was no one in his life like her. She made him remember how it felt to be young again.

Something caught inside his chest, and it had nothing

to do with the injury he'd sustained in his sparring match. Nothing like that. Although an ache was the closest he could come to putting a name to the feeling. And he was pretty sure it had something to do with needing to tell her about London and then saying goodbye.

She started screaming at him to shoot the damn zombies.

Matt managed a smile.

Goddammit. How was he supposed to move to London when he missed her already?

15

MATT WOKE UP SLOWLY, the scent of Sam and sex making him smile before he even opened his eyes. It was early, he knew that, and he hoped Sam was still sleeping. Moving slowly, he reached out to brush her arm, only to find nothing on the mattress but a note.

She'd gone to work. Asked him to call her later, after he was finished with the board meeting. He wasn't a board member, but he did have things he could be doing in the office today. Especially if the vote went his way.

He crumpled the note as he lay back down, smiling at the thought of last night. He and Sam had killed zombies until after midnight, taking just one short break for hot dogs at 9:00 p.m.

It was her fault they'd stayed up until they'd killed the Emperor. He should have called it quits earlier, though—she had a deadline to meet today. But fun won out in the end. He'd had a blast. Both of them were on their feet shooting, yelling, dying, only to start over again. And again. Laughing, too. Jesus, he hadn't laughed so hard in years.

Years. Their adrenaline-fueled sex hadn't lasted long, but it had been smoking hot all the same.

He took in a deep breath and let it out. He would miss her. Far more than he could have ever predicted. Sam had been the best vacation he'd ever had. Was having. It wasn't over yet.

Damn her deadlines. He wanted to spend every minute he could with her. In fact…

He hurried out of bed and into her oddly plain shower, then got dressed. He'd have to stop by the apartment to put on a suit before he could go to the office. But that wouldn't take long. He'd keep the taxi waiting while he changed.

Grabbing his gym bag, hot coffee in hand, he left through Sam's back door. Her lab was right there, a few yards from her house. Like a damn love-struck teenager, he couldn't resist stopping by and seeing her before he left for the office.

Clark answered his buzz. "Oh, great," he said, just loud enough for Matt to hear. "Sorry, but you've missed her."

"Where'd she go?"

"On work-related business. You know we have a killer deadline, and frankly, she looks like shit today. So thanks for that."

"Whoa, hold on there, buddy." Matt walked quickly into the lab before Clark could block him. "Why do you keep breaking my balls?"

"If only," Clark said, not bothering to lower his voice. "You can't wait here. It'll distract everyone, and you'll really throw Sam off her game if you're hanging around."

"I have no intention of *hanging around*. But fine, I'll leave a note. Just…set me up with a piece of paper and an envelope."

"You think I'd read your little love note?"

There were only two other people in the office, as far as he could see—both young women who were now watching them—but Matt didn't care who heard him. Something that should've occurred to him days ago had finally registered. "Are you in love with her?" he asked.

"No." Startled, Clark adjusted his glasses. "I'm not. And neither are you. But that doesn't seem to matter."

"Quit talking in code. Just tell me what's pissing you off," Matt said.

"Let's start with the broken Sam you'll be abandoning. Her crush on you? Remember that little thing?"

Matt made a point of glancing at the two women in the room.

Clark followed his gaze. "Can you guys go work upstairs for a while?" Matt and Clark eyed each other for the minute it took the women to trudge up the stairs.

Then Clark was in his face again. "You don't understand what it took for her to get over her crush. You never saw the repercussions. Mostly because you never bothered to follow up with her. It took her a hell of a long time to get over you, and she's been gun-shy ever since. Then you come along again, and dammit, Wilkinson…" He let out a harsh breath. "Look, Sam can't do it. Okay? She can't."

Matt wasn't sure what he meant by that last statement. But he couldn't bring himself to ask. All he wanted to do was shoot down every point Clark made, but he couldn't do that, either. Matt had worried about the effect this week would have on Sam. Hell, it was doing a number on him, too. "I would never hurt her," he said.

"So this is serious? Wedding serious? You-staying-in-Boston serious?"

That stopped Matt cold. He had no answer. Nothing

was easy about this situation. Mostly, he wondered what Clark had meant when he said Sam couldn't do it. The shitty thing was Matt thought he might know.

Despite all of Sam's assertions that she wasn't a kid anymore, there were parts of her so untested and vulnerable that...

God, what was he going to leave behind when he went to London? At least in New York, she would be just a commuter flight away. London meant jet lag and inconveniently long flights.

"I knew it," Clark said. "Well, congratulations. You've done a good job of making my best friend's life hell. It would serve you right for me to tell her that it was you who paid me to be her watcher."

"Now who wants to do something to hurt her?" Matt said, challenging him.

Clark opened his mouth and shut it quickly. His face paled. Matt didn't even need to turn around to know that Sam had walked in on them. What he didn't know was how much she'd heard.

"You paid Clark to be my watcher? What does that even mean?"

Clark looked at the floor.

Matt turned to Sam. "I wanted him to watch out for you. Logan had already joined the army and Rick and I were about to graduate, and I didn't feel comfortable leaving you alone like that."

"I didn't accept his money after the first year," Clark said.

Sam's eyebrows rose. "Why not?"

"Because I learned so much from you. Because we'd become friends. That's why I'm still here."

"And as my watcher, what exactly were your duties?"

Matt sighed. "You were still having some trouble with time management," he said. "Still skinny as a rail, so you needed someone to remind you about meals and give you a little push to go to class when you got caught up in a project. Nothing major. Just the kind of stuff Logan and Rick and I did for you."

Sam stared at him as if she had no idea what to say. Finally, she just smiled and took his arm. "I'll be back in a few minutes, Clark."

Matt assumed Clark had responded in some nonverbal way. Matt looked at no one but Sam as she led him outside. It was a nice fall day. A little cool, but they were both comfortable in T-shirts.

"How long did you pay Clark?" she asked as they stopped in the shade of the building and she faced him.

"It's like he said—he wouldn't take money after the first year. I'd been in law school for only a few months when he sent the check back." Matt stared at his cold coffee. "Look, I had good intentions—"

"I know you did." She touched his hand. "Frankly, I think it's sweet. I'm impressed that you even gave me a second thought once you left for Harvard."

"Of course I did. You know why I'd made myself scarce in those months leading up to it. We talked about it yesterday."

"I know." She was studying him closely and making him nervous. "I have a question, and please answer honestly."

Time to man up. "Ask me anything."

"Why did you want me to go to the gala with you?"

Matt frowned. It was the last question he'd expected. "I don't know what to say to that. Where is this coming from? You know why."

"I don't care if asking me was politically motivated. I really don't. I had a good time with you. I'm just curious."

Jesus. Now Matt understood. "You heard my father's asinine comment."

"I did." She winced. "I walked away once I knew neither of you had seen me."

Great. Just friggin' great. Sam had to be wondering about all the other secrets he was keeping from her.

Man, he sure would've liked to punch something now.

SAM KNEW INSTANTLY that she'd hurt him. That was the thing with intimacy. She could tell when he was hurt. And when he was angry. Now it was both.

"I took you to the gala because you're my friend. I wanted your support and your company. Anything apart from that never crossed my mind. Ever." He shook his head, an expression of pure disgust on his face. "I know I'm not as smart as you. Jesus, who is? But I've proved my worth to my father and to the company. I don't need you or anyone else as a prop."

Sam lowered her lashes, then rallied to meet his eyes. "That's not what I meant. I know you're smart, and you're terrific at your job. I just… Galas aren't the kind of thing I'm usually asked to. I apologize." She touched his arm, trying to let him see she was being sincere.

He pulled her into his arms. "It's not enough that you're beautiful, successful, brilliant and that I wouldn't have wanted anyone at my side more than you? I'm so proud of you, Sammy. Everything about you. Not just your brains."

"When I heard your dad—"

"You clearly didn't hear me snapping back at him. I swear, Sam—"

"No." She put a finger on his lips. "Don't say anything more. You don't have to."

He moved her hand and kissed her fears away, and when she remembered how he'd actually hired Clark to watch over her? If he hadn't been holding her up, she'd have melted right into the ground.

When she kissed him back, she heard his moan. Sadly, it didn't last. Matt pulled back.

"As much as I'd like to do this for the rest of the day, I have to get to the office. There are some issues that…" He stopped, smiled. "Sorry—I just need to be there to see what they've done this time."

"Don't worry about it. I've got to get back to work."

"How about we meet up for dinner?"

"It might have to be really late."

"No problem. I'll call you, okay?"

She nodded. "Go before I can't help myself and kiss you again."

"That's no way to chase me away. But I'll go," he said, walking backward. "Despite the fact that you're a better zombie killer than I'll ever be."

"What a guy," she said, watching him sidestep a tree. "You're much better about losing than you were the last time we played."

"When you're the consolation prize? I could have lost a hundred games and still come out the winner." He bumped into a shrub. "Ouch. I'll call you," he repeated.

She bit her lip. "After the meeting, do you think you'll know more about when you'll be leaving?" She blurted it out, not even sure she wanted to know the answer.

Matt looked startled. Probably sick of her fixating on the subject. "For London?"

London? "No, New York."

"Oh. No. Probably won't know for several days, at least."

"Okay. 'Bye. Talk to you later." She watched him jog to the curb, willing her heart to slow its furious beat, but how could she, knowing they still had some time? The London thing had rattled him. Why, she wasn't sure. She knew he traveled a lot. Japan, Germany. England. But there had been an odd moment.

She turned, aware that anyone could've been watching them kiss from the windows. She should have cared, but the thought actually made her walk taller as she headed back inside. She needed to have a word with Clark.

He was there, just as she'd figured. Waiting with a hazelnut latte for her, which wasn't going to get him out of this mess. She asked him to follow her to her office and to close the door behind him, something that was rarely done during work hours.

"So this is a problem," she said. "He's not even going to be here for much longer. Do you have to antagonize him every time? I still don't get what you're so pissed about. The guy hired you to watch over me. We became friends because of him, and it's been the most amazing twelve years ever."

"I know that." Clark put the cup down and crossed his arms over his chest. Not the best sign that he was going to back down. "I don't like that he's going to leave. You know he won't keep in contact with you. He barely texted you after he went off to Harvard. And when he did just now, it was so he could use the apartment."

"You don't know that."

"I know people don't change. He married a freaking model. He travels to Asia and Europe all the time. I read he's going to get his trust-fund money in a year or so, and then who knows? He might quit working and become an international playboy."

"A little wish fulfillment there, Clark?"

"What? No. Well, yeah. Maybe. But my point stands. He's going to leave, and you're going to be a mess. Don't even try to tell me you won't be. I've got eyes. I see you're in love with him. And I don't begrudge you that. If he was living in Boston, if he didn't have the Wilkinson name…if he was just a regular guy, I'd be all for it. Hell, I'd help plan the damn wedding. But he's—"

"Out of my league?"

"No." He took a deep breath and exhaled loudly. Then met her eyes. "Maybe. Not for the reasons you're thinking, though. I just—I don't like seeing you get hurt, and he's going to hurt you, whether he means to or not. You deserve so much more."

"Well, then, it's a good thing I'm married to my work. Look, I appreciate the concern. I do. But having you scowling and angry at Matt doesn't help. I'll be fine. And if I'm not, then I'm going to need my best friend. But I won't come to you if all you're going to do is tell me that you told me so."

"I'd never do that."

"And I'm pretty sure Matt's not going to forget about me the day he leaves Boston. Until then, if he happens to come by, please be nicer to him. Although I doubt he will. Please, Clark. We've got too much work to do for me to worry about this."

Clark nodded. "Okay. I know I've said before that I'll back off and I haven't, but I will. And I'll assume that Matt's intentions are good."

"Thank you. I mean it. And now I need that coffee if I'm going to get out of here before midnight."

"Fair enough."

Clark handed over her coffee and went to the door. Just as he grabbed the handle, Sam said, "Did you notice that bruise on his chin?"

"Yeah. It looked like it would hurt."

With a straight face, she said, "You should have seen the other guy."

Clark's eyes widened as he realized what she meant.

She smiled when she turned her back so she could reheat her latte.

It wasn't until early evening that Matt left the Wilkinson building, shell-shocked. He'd made his father repeat the fact that the vote had not only been in Matt's favor... it had been unanimous.

His arm went out as if pulled by a string, and a taxi appeared at the curb. Matt could have been entering a spaceship for all he cared.

How was this his life now?

He got out his cell and speed-dialed Sam, noticing how late it was. Luckily, he'd texted her at some point to give her fair warning. Her text back, just the word GREAT in all caps, meant she was running late, as well. She picked up on the first ring. "Hey. Are you still working?"

"Just left," he said. "How about you?"

"Forever and ever," she said, followed by a long sigh.

"That doesn't sound good. Shall I wait at the apartment?"

"That's probably best. I really shouldn't be too much longer."

"I gotta tell you something real quick—either the board was impressed that I knew you or they've finally realized I'm actually a damn good attorney. They voted

unanimously to put me in charge of the London office."
He paused. No reaction. Of course she wouldn't get it.
He'd explain later. "Most of those guys are old-school.
Getting a unanimous vote is un-friggin'-believable."

The driver turned with an impatient glare. "Yo, man.
Where to?"

"Sam, can you hold for a sec?" He pulled the phone
away and gave the man the address.

Then he was back with Sam. "I'll explain all the details later. But I'd like to take you somewhere really special. I can get us a nine o'clock reservation at the chef's
table at L'Espalier if you like French. Or Grotto if you'd
prefer Italian. I know the chef at the Wilkinson would
knock our socks off, as well, so just say the word."

He heard something in the background, but because of
the noise on the street, he couldn't make out any words.
For all he knew, Sam wasn't on the line. Probably multi-
tasking.

Finally, she came back. "I'm really sorry," she said,
sounding frantic. "I've got to put you on hold for a minute."

"Sure—"

She'd already put him on hold.

He stared out the window as they drove, his mind flying in a thousand different directions. He tried to focus
on dinner and wondered where else she might like to go.
Maybe he should have suggested Chinese. He knew she
liked it, but the best of the best wasn't nearly as romantic as he wanted.

If she didn't have a preference, he'd take her to the
hotel. See if maybe they could get a room there. A suite.
Yeah, that would be—

"Matt? You still there?"

"Yeah, I am. I—"

"Listen, I'm sorry, but I've got an emergency on my hands here. I promise we'll have a celebratory dinner as soon as possible, but tonight's not going to work. I'm sorry."

"Well, wait. We can eat late."

"Sorry."

"But I'll still see you tonight?"

"I have to go. I'll call," she said and disconnected.

Matt blinked a few times and stared at the phone as if it could tell him what the hell was going on. He had no idea what to do. He hadn't even got to the part where he'd turned down the promotion.

Talk about a letdown.

It wasn't her fault. She hadn't planned the emergency. He understood. Work came first.

He stared at the people crowding the sidewalks, the cars with impatient drivers weaving in and out of traffic. The sky was blue and tinged with twilight, a perfect fall evening. He glanced at his watch, then checked his phone for messages he might've missed. Nothing.

His mind wouldn't settle.

Okay, so he hadn't mentioned London before now, and that might've annoyed her. He'd planned to tell her everything at dinner. Something he still intended to do, so she'd understand why he'd been tight-lipped. Hopefully, she'd be pleased with the final outcome and that would take care of everything else.

But thinking about it, he honestly wasn't sure she'd even heard or processed what he had said. If he thought it wouldn't annoy the crap out of her, he'd call right now and straighten things out, but she'd sounded so harried. But he'd have another chance to explain later.

The last-minute decision he'd made would change his life dramatically. He'd deeply disappointed his father. The board that had just given him the ultimate vote of confidence would be blindsided. Matt had set aside his whole career for Sam. For them.

Then again, they'd never discussed their relationship. In fact, the only thing they had agreed upon was that they were both incredibly busy people, both immersed in their careers. When Clark had called him on his intentions toward Sam, Matt had been at a total loss. That should've been a damn big clue.

He laid his head back and closed his eyes.

Jesus. Now was a hell of a time to have second thoughts. Why hadn't he talked to Sam first before he'd turned down the opportunity of a lifetime?

He thought about calling his father and telling him he'd reconsidered, then immediately scratched that foolish notion. Why add another stupidly impulsive decision to the mess? He was probably overreacting anyway.

Sam had a work emergency. That was all.

A nagging voice reminded him that was how it would always be.

For her.

And for him.

So what the hell kind of chance would they have anyway?

16

SAM KNEW ENOUGH to keep breathing. She had a tendency to hold her breath until she got dizzy when panicking, and she wasn't going to let that happen. Matt's time-out to talk to the driver had allowed her to gather her wits. At least, enough to put him on hold before she'd said something she would regret.

He hadn't told her about London. Not about taking over the office, not that the board had to vote for him to get the position. Nothing. He'd removed her from his personal life as neatly as Arthur pulled Excalibur from the stone.

She'd known their new relationship wouldn't last. From day one. But ending it like this? With a blithe comment from the back of a taxi? What on earth was there to celebrate? He could damn well congratulate himself on his new job.

God, how had she been so utterly wrong?

The answer was simple. Because she was so bad at this stuff. Always had been. She was an idiot to have believed she'd magically changed just because Prince Charming had paid her a little attention. So yeah, she was partly to blame for this, but not for all of it.

What she couldn't figure out was why he hadn't told her. Did he think she wouldn't want to see him if she knew he was moving to London? They were supposedly friends. People who shared things about their lives. He'd stayed in her apartment, come to her lab, invited her to the gala.

She'd spent the night with him. Twice. Once in her own house.

If she had the power to do anything, it would be to take that back. No. She'd need to start at the beginning. The day he called from New York. She could have told him any story in the world, and he wouldn't have known. She could have kept her distance, kept her heart intact.

"Hey," Clark said, coming to her side. "You okay?"

She managed a smile. "Yes. Sorry. Just thinking."

"You sure? I thought you and Matt were going to go out tonight."

"There's too much work to do. Which is what I was thinking about. I'm pretty sure if we take a look at the second set of protocols, we'll find a repeat error."

"Oh." Clark stood still for a moment. "That would explain…"

He wandered off and she thanked whatever source had given her that Hail Mary thought.

She wanted to go outside. To run until she had no breath left. To submerge herself in her tub until things didn't hurt as much. She'd been so sure she could handle this thing with Matt, even his leaving.

After everything that had happened, how was it that she was still that heartbroken sixteen-year-old girl?

STANDING AT THE window in his father's office, Matt stared at his phone, listening to the now-memorized message from Sam to leave his name and number. He wanted to throw the damn thing across the room.

It was Tuesday afternoon, almost twenty-two hours since he'd called her from the taxi, and everything was fucked up.

The entire board of directors was furious at him, and not an insignificant number of staff. His "stunt," as Uncle Frank had so charmingly called it, wasn't appreciated. He'd made them look like fools.

Terrance Bannister had held his voice just below the level of a shout the whole place could hear when he'd accused Matt of undermining the board and the whole company, by not letting them pursue legitimate candidates for the London office.

Now they were in an emergency session, scrambling to find his replacement. He'd get only one chance to redeem himself to the board and, more important, his father, and that chance had been given reluctantly. He imagined they wanted to fill up the few hours he'd asked for yelling at him some more.

He debated waiting to have coffee in the boardroom. He needed it. Sleep had been as elusive as Sam. A bottle of water would be better for him, but no. He had time to go to the lounge and get a strong hot cup there before heading to the gallows.

Where the hell was she? Why wasn't she picking up his calls? Calling him back? He got that work was probably crazy, but to hang him out to dry like this? He wanted to tell her everything, and she had given him nothing. Not even the courtesy of a damn phone call.

What if he didn't hear from her again? What if he'd

given up the chance for London, all for nothing? What if this ache in his heart was here to stay? He'd been so sure…

Upon entering the lounge, he felt eyes shift away from him and a few people actually left. He quietly made his coffee, itching to check his messages one more time. But he wouldn't. In fact, the moment he walked into the boardroom, he would turn off his phone for as long as it took to share the entire plan he'd designed for the London office.

His steps were heavy on the thick pile carpet. He'd never felt anything but welcome in these halls. This was where he'd grown up, as much as the house on Beacon Hill. He'd worked here summers, channeled his love of puzzles into an unshakable goal in the library. He'd admired his father so much.

Now Matt would either prove that his instincts were right or disgrace not just himself but the man who'd raised him.

No one said a word as he entered the room. A screen was set up for his PowerPoint presentation. He checked his phone one last time before shutting it down, and he made the decision that if he didn't hear from Sam by the time he'd finished his talk, he'd make his reservation for New York.

"Gentlemen," he said. "Here's how I believe we can take the London office to the next level."

For the next two hours and twenty-four minutes, Matt laid it all out. Beginning with a reassessment of their goals, a status update and a step-by-step plan to change the trajectory of the eighty-seven employees who worked at that office. Many of their best people had taken off for brighter shores, and Matt had an idea about how they could attract them back.

It was a remarkably quiet reception. The questions aimed at him were sharp, on point. By the time his presentation was over, all the coffee was gone and exhaustion was sneaking up his spine. Matt wanted more than anything to leave. To escape what should have been a triumphant moment. But he wasn't even sure he'd landed his punches.

Bannister cleared his voice, being the first to break the silence. "I still think what you did was rotten," he said, "and that will continue to be a disappointment, but it's clear you've put a tremendous amount of thought and preparation into this plan of yours. With the right person at the helm, I believe you've outlined the best course of action. One that, I agree, will bring London back from the breech."

Matt held in his grateful sigh. "Thank you" was all he said. Then it was up to the rest of the board to chime in. And chime in they did. None of them wanted to change much about his plan, but they all wanted to change a little. He understood. They wanted to leave their mark, and to call his presentation an unequivocal success after his bailing on them would have been too much.

As it was, he was the lone voice calling for the retention of the current manager, Stephen Fairchild. Matt felt Fairchild had the right stuff, just the wrong target for his talents.

They wouldn't consider it. At least, not when Matt was in the room.

Finally, he agreed that he would fly to London to clean house. He'd lay the groundwork and be there for whoever was going to run the office. He wouldn't commit to when he would leave, not until he checked his phone. Thankfully, his father cut off the line of questioning.

Then he was freed. Keeping it together, he packed up his things and left the room. His first stop was the bathroom, where he found zero messages left on his voice mail. No texts, either.

He didn't even really have the right to be mad. Only sad. Being with Sam had changed him so much it seemed incredible that she hadn't changed, as well, but he had the evidence before him.

She must have had a reason to blow him off like this. Maybe Clark had got to her, convinced her that making a clean break was her best option. But it didn't sound like Sam to be swayed that drastically. She'd at least hear him out. He'd been clear in his messages to her that he had much more to tell her. That he wanted to explain in person, not in a voice mail.

Before all this, they had been friends. Now he doubted they ever would be again. After pouring yet one more cup of coffee in the thankfully empty lounge, he headed for his father's office, where he found his old man sitting behind his desk. "You did an excellent job with the plans. I think you'll get through this change of course very well."

Matt sat and stared at the law books that lined the built-in shelves. He let his father's compliment sink in. He'd worked a long time for it. None of his planning had been on company time. He'd strategized for months, quietly, patiently. He'd privately tried to share his concept with Fairchild, but his input hadn't been welcomed. It was clear he saw Matt not only as his competition but as a dilettante instead of a valuable part of Wilkinson Holdings.

"Thank you," Matt said finally, straightening to face his father.

"The only thing I'm not sure about is your idea to keep Fairchild on."

"Clearly that's up to you and the board. It was just a suggestion."

"I'll consider it further. Now, what are your immediate plans?"

Jesus. Matt hoped he wasn't about to suggest a family dinner. "Call Andrew. Check up on the Tokyo deal and make sure Budapest is on target."

"Not seeing Ms. O'Connel?"

"No. She's got some serious deadlines to face. I took up a lot of time she didn't really have."

His father nodded. "You might want to set up shop in Stanley's old office today and tomorrow. Let the board members talk to you. It'll go a long way toward smoothing things out."

"I will. And thanks. For the support. It means a lot."

"I'm still not thrilled about the way you handled things."

Matt smiled. "I know. I would have done things differently, given the chance."

Charles cleared his throat, his attention moving to a folder on his desk.

Matt left the office, prepared as he'd ever be for the verbal floggings he was about to receive.

He wouldn't call Sam again.

MATT CALLED SAM four more times. He'd got the same message each time. At least he'd slept for about five hours, which was a hell of a lot better than he'd done the night before. When he'd left this morning, he'd taken his things with him and checked into the Wilkinson Hotel. It hadn't felt right to be in Sam's apartment anymore.

He'd miss the place. It had Sam's unique stamp on it. But the best part of all had been Sam. Eating waffles together. Her naked, in his arms. The way she'd gone all supertech when they'd discovered that sex tape. Hell, everything they'd done had been amazing. Didn't matter if it was getting a couples massage, shooting zombies or making her blush in the shower.

So what had gone wrong? He couldn't get past the part where he'd been so *sure*. Sure that she wanted what he wanted. More time together. With an eye toward a life together. He didn't know how they'd get there, but it would be criminal not to try.

But he guessed he was the only one who'd felt that way.

He'd had a few more conversations with members of the board that afternoon. At least people weren't avoiding him any longer, for which he should have felt grateful, but all he wanted was to be left on his own. To figure out what to do next.

The only thing he could think to do was catch her at the lab and ask for a face-to-face. He hoped it wouldn't feel like an ambush—it certainly wasn't his first choice. But it could be the only chance he'd have to talk to her. Before he left, however, there were two things he needed to do: book himself a flight to New York and say goodbye to his father. The first was over in a matter of minutes, but when he stopped by his father's office, Charles asked him to come in and shut the door behind him.

"What's wrong? Are you all right?"

"I'm fine," Charles said. "I've noticed that you're not

yourself, though, son. That's understandable, but something tells me it has nothing to do with work."

Matt sighed. He didn't want to go into detail, but he was relieved to share some of what had happened with another human being. "It's Sam. She cut me off. Hasn't responded to my phone calls, and I don't know why. It probably has something to do with me not telling her about London to begin with. I'm not sure."

His father nodded and gave a small smile at the last part. "I'm afraid I can't help you with that, except to offer some advice, if it would be welcome."

"Of course it would."

"You told me the reason you were going to pass on the London office was because of your changed relationship with Samantha. For what it's worth, I think you made the right decision."

"She won't even talk to me."

"If she was just a friend, she would have. It would all be easy. My advice is for you to go with your heart. Do what you need to do to find out what's bothering her. There will always be a place for you in the company, or any first-class law firm, but a woman as formidable as Samantha O'Connel? I did some reading about her. She's quite a phenomenon."

"She is. But that's not the reason I want—"

"I believe you. In my life I have a few regrets that have never truly left me. When I was a young man, I had a similar opportunity, but I chose the well-beaten path. The safe road. Between you and me, given the chance, I would have done things differently."

Matt recognized the echo of his own words, but that was nothing compared to the confession his father had just made. He considered their relationship to be a very good one, but they'd never been confidants. It was an exceptional admission, one that helped Matt know that going to Sam was the right move.

"I'm proud of you, son. You've never had to prove yourself to me, yet you've done that over and over again. Give yourself every opportunity to live a full life. That will make me proud, as well."

Matt stood up. He wasn't going to hug his father or anything. God, they'd probably both have heart attacks. But he did offer his hand. His father stood and accepted it. And he clapped Matt on the shoulder.

"Thank you," Matt said, swallowing around the lump in his throat.

When he reached the office door, his father said, "Good luck." That carried him all the way to a taxi and straight on to Sam's lab.

She wasn't there.

Clark stepped outside, not even letting Matt see past the door. "She hasn't been here for two days," Clark said, anger and worry in his voice. "I warned you this would happen, but did you listen? No. She hasn't missed a day since I can remember. She's devastated."

"Devastated? But why? I haven't done anything—"

"Bullshit. You were on the phone with her, and when she hung up, she looked like a ghost. Her hands were shaking so badly she couldn't finish the page she was working on."

"Wait a minute. Just wait. What did she say? Exactly."

"Nothing. She wouldn't talk to me. Something else she's never done before." Clark blinked and adjusted his glasses. "I know she feels miserable and humiliated."

Matt ran a hand through his hair as he turned around. "She didn't let me finish," he said.

"What?"

He turned back to Clark. "Christ. I was in a cab. The board of directors had just voted for me to take over the London office. Huge deal. I'd been working toward the promotion for a year."

"Well, that explains—"

Matt cut him off. "No. It explains nothing because she never heard the rest. I turned the job down. My father, the rest of the board, everyone was furious with me. I can barely believe I did it. I did it for her. For us. To see if we could have a chance. But she didn't return any of my calls."

Clark looked stunned. He didn't do anything but stare for a long minute. Then, "Shit."

Matt inhaled. "You can say that again. What do I do now? Do you know if she's at home?"

"You really turned down the job?"

"Of course I did. It's Sam."

"Try her again," Clark said. Then he shook his head as if he were clearing out cobwebs. "Come in." He held the door for Matt, who was already dialing her number.

He disconnected. "Straight to voice mail."

Clark pulled his phone out of his pocket. "Hey, Sam. How are you doing? Good." He gave a small shake of his head. "I know you said not to bother you, but I have something to tell you. It's important. So please hear me out. I've talked to Matt— No. Just listen." Clark tightened his mouth. "I don't think it's the flu, Sam. Okay. Even if it is, it won't hurt you to give Matt a call back."

Matt wanted to tear his hair out, not being able to hear what she was saying. All he could do was hope.

"No, you're not listening. I've talked to him. He didn't

get to finish what he was saying to you the other day. He didn't take the London job. He turned it down."

Silence.

Second by second, Clark's expression darkened, his shoulders slumped, and finally, he had to turn his back on Matt. A few moments later Clark hung up.

"What happened?"

"I'm sorry," Clark said, looking bleak. "She said that even though you didn't take the job, nothing has changed. You have your work, she has hers. You're both busy people and have different lives. And she's known that all along."

"But none of that is written in stone. We could try. I don't want her to quit her job. But I don't want her missing out on life, either."

"I know, man. I get it. I've never heard her like this before. I don't know what to tell you." Clark took off his glasses and rubbed his eyes. "Oh, and she says being AWOL has nothing to do with you. She has the flu. And she'll call you when she feels better."

Matt reached into his pocket for the key to the apartment. "Dammit," he muttered under his breath. "She thinks she has everything all figured out."

Looking dejected, Clark accepted the key.

Matt felt himself sinking deeper. Maybe he was the one who wasn't thinking straight. He'd taken a risk, and it hadn't paid off. He might be able to get the London gig back, but it wouldn't mean much. Considering what he'd just lost.

He just couldn't think of anything more he could do. Other than finding out if she was home and breaking down her front door.

God knew he'd had worse ideas.

17

Sam sank to her couch, dropping her cell phone on the coffee table. She felt wretched. She hadn't done much to make herself feel better. That wouldn't happen for another decade or so. At least she'd showered this morning. Cried the whole time.

She wished Clark hadn't told her. It was easier to stay strong when there was the whole London Secret to hold on to. The fact that he'd turned down the job was...

She wasn't sure what to think. Maybe it was because of her, but probably not. Or he would've said something in one of his many messages.

Dammit. What was Matt talking to Clark for, anyway? So they were suddenly buddies now? This wasn't anyone's business. The employees thought she had the flu. Honestly, it felt like the flu, only much worse.

Sniffling, she inhaled a calming breath. If Matt thought he'd be seeing more of her by staying, he was asking for the impossible. He might as well have accepted the London job. He traveled so often that taking over the office felt like only a technicality. And her life was all about her work. She spent eighty, ninety hours a week in the lab. It could never work between them. Someone's heart would end up broken. It was only a matter of time.

So why had she let things get this far? She couldn't blame all of this on him.

God, how she must have driven Clark insane. At least they'd completed the Coulson job.

She got up and shuffled to the kitchen. Normally, she loved her kitchen. Pictures and magnets took up most of the room on the front of the fridge. She had the same espresso machine as the office, and it made the best hazelnut lattes in the world. She also had a shiny bright red toaster and a red butter dish and her whole Le Creuset baking set was red. A gift in happier days. Not that she baked anything but macaroni and cheese.

Making coffee was easy enough on autopilot. Her hair needed to be out of her face, but she hadn't wanted to look in a mirror, so she'd avoided the bathroom.

Even a great challenge on "World of Warcraft" hadn't lifted her spirits one bit. Maybe a dash of Kahlúa would liven up her coffee. More than a dash sounded even better.

She wondered when Clark had talked to Matt and whether or not it had been in person. She hadn't thought to ask, but she wouldn't have anyway. It didn't matter. Except that she wanted to know. Maybe she could brush her hair. Try to hide whatever damage there was from crying so much. Put on some jeans. Casually walk over and see if Clark would tell her more without her asking.

But why?

It was just…

She missed Matt. So, so much. She'd had such a short time with him, yet he'd managed to infiltrate every part of her. She would have thought something so encompassing would stifle her creativity, but it hadn't. She'd come up with the solution to the power problem in record time.

Making herself move, she finished her coffee. There were muffins in the fridge. And in the freezer. But eating seemed like a horrible idea.

So back to the couch it was, where she could wallow to her heart's content.

Although she doubted there was any heart left.

MATT MADE IT as far as the street and turned around. He wasn't a quitter, and damned if he was going to throw in the towel on something this important. The lab's front door opened, and for a moment, his heart almost beat out of his chest, but it was the assistant. Tina. She nodded at him with a smile and gave Clark a subtle questioning look.

Clark walked over and stood next to her, a protective hand on the small of her back. "I don't know what more I can do," he said, keeping his voice low.

"I'm not letting her wimp out of this. Being with her helped me reconnect with a part of me that I lost in law school. I've laughed more in the last week than in the last year. It helped me see that my schedule was nuts.

"I think the same goes for Sam. And you, too. Life is more than work, even if it's creative and satisfying. I got my ass kicked two ways to Sunday when we played 'House of the Dead' the other night. She was jumping around and screaming like a kid on spring break."

Clark nodded. "Even though I was a complete downer through this whole thing, she was happier than I'd seen her in ages."

"Look, I have an idea, but first I need to know if you

think you guys could keep on running things without Sam for three more days."

Clark looked back at Tina, who met his gaze with wide eyes and a small smile. "Yeah, we'd be okay," he said. "Now that we're finished with the Coulson job, things are more or less back to normal."

"What about your schedule?"

"I've already padded that, and most of our clients are cool with time." Clark reached for the apartment key he'd left on his desk. "What do you have in mind?"

"For starters, I won't need that. If I play this right, Sam will be leaving town with me tonight."

"You're kidding, right?" Clark once again stole a glance at Tina. "I don't know about that. You'd be lucky to get her to leave the house, let alone leave town with you."

"Aside from going out the back way, there's one more thing."

"Okay." Clark followed and almost ran into him when Matt stopped. They'd reached the middle of the lab floor, right near Tina's desk. "So what's the other thing?"

"If she won't let me in, can one of you help me out? Maybe pretend to take something over to her. I don't want to have to bust down the door."

A collective sigh floated down from somewhere above them. Matt looked up. Three young women were hanging over the loft railing, apparently listening to everything.

Matt pointed to them. "None of you warn Sam. Please."

All three heads nodded solemnly.

"If you can't get her to open the door, I could probably figure something out," Tina said softly, then glanced again at Clark, who was staring at her. "Whatever we can do," she said, then looked back at Matt. "We're in."

"Thanks." Matt studied the other man for a moment. "You know, Clark, a very wise and successful man told me that he regretted letting work take over his life. Given the chance, he would do things differently. I intend to not make his mistakes. And I won't let Sam do it, either. One way or another, I'll convince her. Because neither one of us should have any regrets about what might have been. There's a time for bold moves, and now is that time."

Clark inhaled, gave him a short nod and took off his glasses. "You're right," he said, before he turned his full attention on Tina and pulled her into one mother of a kiss.

Shouts and cheers erupted from upstairs and the break room. Matt smiled, but this wasn't his party.

Once outside, Matt got on the phone with his assistant. As he walked across the very long yard, he explained what he needed. If no commercial flights were available, he'd use the company jet, something he rarely did. When he reached her door, Matt took a deep breath and knocked firmly.

When about a minute had gone by and she hadn't come to the door, he knocked again. With conviction. And then he did it a third time.

Thank God, the door swung open.

"What do you want, Matt?"

He smiled at how beautiful she looked. Her hair was a wild mess, as though she'd just got up after spending the night with him. Her beige thermal shirt couldn't hide the fact that she wasn't wearing a bra, and she had on funky red-and-white pajama bottoms. Her feet were bare, her silver-polished toes curled against the brisk air. "I need you to get dressed and pack a bag for a three-day trip. Casual clothes will be fine, but maybe throw in a couple of nice things."

Her jaw dropped. She just squinted at him through red-rimmed eyes and didn't say anything.

He smiled.

Eventually, she said, "Are you crazy? Even if I wanted to go anywhere with you, there's no way I'd leave Clark to handle everything."

"Why not? According to him, they've done fine without you for the last two days and three more won't matter. And once he and Tina come up for air, I'm sure he'll be happy to confirm that for you."

Sam frowned. "Come up for air?"

Matt nodded and started herding her back into the living room.

HE KEPT SMILING at her as if he had a big happy surprise waiting for her. As if everything were just peachy.

"Stop it," she said, slapping at his hands.

"Hold that thought." He pulled his cell phone out of his jacket pocket and read a text. Once he'd put it away, he said, "I can help you pack if you want, but our flight leaves in two hours, so we have to hustle."

"I'm not going anywhere with— Wait. Clark and Tina?"

"Kissing. Yes. Very enthusiastically. Everyone seemed to be pleased about it."

"Everyone?"

"He kissed her at her desk."

She sighed. Her latte was still on the coffee table, and suddenly, drinking it was the only thing that made sense. Besides, she didn't want Matt to see her lower lip wobble. Clark and Tina had kissed and she hadn't been there.

"Where are you going? That's not your bedroom."

"First of all, stop it. Second…" She didn't complete

her thought. A long drink of the now-not-so-hot latte helped. "Second, where do you think you're taking me? Although from what I can see, thinking is the last thing you seem to be doing."

He looked down at his feet for a minute, and she hid again behind her tall mug. He looked worn-out. There were dark shadows under his eyes that told her he hadn't been sleeping, either. Of course, he'd done that to himself, but it still broke her heart. Seeing him was opening the wound again, before it had even started to heal.

"I know you turned down the job in London. I really hope it didn't have anything to do with me, because it doesn't matter where you live. We can't be together. You're delusional if you think it's possible. Do you know how much time I wasted this last week alone?"

"Yeah," he said. "None. Zero. There wasn't one damn moment of wasted time between us. Tell me you didn't have a great time."

"Just because something's fun and wonderful doesn't make it all right. I've got responsibilities."

"So do I. And if I thought there wasn't an excellent chance that we could work this thing out, I never would have turned down the promotion. I mean it, Sam. We have a lot to talk about. I know that. But I'm asking you to take it on faith that you'll be glad you packed for three days."

"On faith? Why didn't you tell me about London? You never even mentioned it, and I don't understand."

He took a deep breath, but he didn't look away. "I didn't mean to hide it from you. In the beginning I had no idea what the board was going to do. In fact, it didn't look so good. Then when things started to shift, I didn't want to tell you, because there was still a chance it wouldn't have gone my way."

"So?"

"Dammit, Sam. I didn't want to fail in front of you like that."

"Fail? Oh, for God's sake, Matthew. You're a damn good lawyer and you're too smart to think you had to prove anything to me, remember?"

He smiled. "Yes. I remember. But when something is as important as you are, I wanted to make sure all my ducks were in a row."

"That doesn't make any sense. Not with me it doesn't. We're friends first. At least, I like to think so." She couldn't stand to think how awful she looked. Every time she sniffed, she imagined her nose growing redder and redder. It probably matched her hair by now. "So how did the board react to you turning the job down?"

"They haven't taken out any hits on me, as far as I know. But they're not thrilled. I've outlined all the changes I'd hoped to implement, though. Everything necessary to restructure and come back swinging. I'll have to go there for a couple of weeks, get everything rolling in the right direction. But I don't have to go yet."

It took her a minute to digest what he'd just told her. She stood there, sipping her drink, looking at this insane man who'd turned down his dream. What must that have been like? To tell his father must have taken all the courage in the world. And now he wanted to take even more time off to show her some little surprise? "Should you even dare to leave now?"

"Yes. I've got something more important to do." He checked his watch and then sighed again. "Can we argue about this later? Like on the plane? Seriously, you need to pack now."

"What on earth is going away for three days going to do but put us both further behind?"

"Dammit, Sam. Life isn't only about work. I've been as guilty as you, working so many hours that I lost all sense of time and priorities. But being with you again has changed things. Remember how much gaming we did in the dorm?"

"Of course I do, but—"

"We still aced our classes, didn't we? And those were some hard classes. Well, not necessarily for you, but that's not the point. We used to have fun and work hard. We had lives outside of our books and midterms."

Sam just stared at him, not sure what to say. Kind of ironic, really, that she wanted to be the grown-up and here she was, acting the part. But Matt, he'd never been the pie-in-the-sky type. She didn't doubt for a minute he believed they could find some common ground, have a slice of life together. But once they returned to their real lives, it was going to become more and more difficult to carve out time for each other. She just couldn't see this story having a happy ending.

Matt took her empty mug and put it back on the coffee table. From there, he took hold of both of her hands. "I understand that you love what you do. I love what I do, too. But is that all there can be to life? I don't think so. No, scratch that. I *know* it isn't, and I'm asking you to trust me for a little while. A few days? If you're still not convinced we have a chance, then consider the matter dropped. Never to be broached again. You have my word."

What he was asking for felt too big for her to give. But she also wouldn't be able to live with herself if she didn't at least try.

She managed a nod. "I'll go pack."

18

THEY WERE LANDING at JFK Airport and Sam still wasn't
sure if she was making a horrible mistake or if Matt
really did know what he was doing. She tried not to let
her pessimism show, and so far, they hadn't talked about
anything of consequence on the short trip. Recollections
from their shared past, mostly. Good memories, funny
things. Games they'd played and comics they'd read.

At this point, there was only one thing she knew for
certain. She couldn't possibly fall any more in love with
Matt. She'd reached heights her young self had never
imagined as she'd got to know him again.

But it was very clear, at least to her, that she might
have been simply delaying the inevitable heartbreak. And
the tragic irony of it all? When everything went up in
smoke, work would be her solace and her hiding place.

Eventually, she'd get over him, and life as she'd known
it for at least the past four years would return.

"I've got a car waiting for us," he said.

"You're still not going to tell me where we're going?"

"Nope."

She bit her lower lip and gripped the seat arms as they

approached the runway. After the jolt of the landing, she could breathe again. "You know," she said as they were rolling to the gate, "Midtown is going to be extra busy. New York Comic Con is happening this week."

"No kidding?" He shrugged. "The city is always crowded."

The seat-belt sign went off, causing half the passengers around them to spring up and get their luggage before the door was open. Matt among them. First class wasn't too bad, though. They'd deplane first.

"Come on, slowpoke," Matt urged. He had both their carry-on bags and was hogging the aisle.

She got in back of him and followed him off the plane and into the mellow chaos of the terminal. As soon as they stepped past the security point, a driver was there to greet them. He took the bags from Matt. The young man wasn't wearing a uniform, but his suit was impeccable. "I've gone over my instructions with your assistant, Mr. Wilkinson. So if you'd follow me, please?"

His name was Diego, and he whisked them out of the airport like a champ. The car was a luxury black sedan, something stately that she'd never buy in a million years, even if she liked to drive.

"So what now?" she asked, settling in the backseat. "A blindfold? A bag over my head?"

"How about we make out until we get there?"

She looked in the rearview and met Diego's dark brown gaze, which he shifted immediately. "I'd have to be a little drunk to do that."

"Are you sure?" Matt leaned in, smiling. "Then how about a kiss? Just one," he said. "Then we renegotiate."

She was here, he looked happy, and she'd missed him so very much over two horrible days. Her hand went to one of her favorite places—his nape—and she brushed her fingers over his soft dark hair. "I missed you."

He nodded. "I think my incessant phone messages were an indication of how much I missed you. I'm so sorry our conversation got hijacked, but even sorrier that I didn't tell you about what was going on with London in the first place."

"I forgive you. For both things," she said, not that she thought it changed anything. But he already knew how she felt. No need to hit him over the head with it.

In the front seat, Diego cleared his throat. "We've arrived."

Sam, who hadn't been paying attention to anything but Matt, said, "How are we here? We were hardly in the car."

"JFK isn't that far from the Javits Center," Matt said.

"But that's—" She inhaled a gasp. "Comic Con? That's where you're taking me?"

"Yep."

"Okay, now I really need to know what the heck is going on."

"We're going to Comic Con," Matt said patiently. "What more explanation do you need?"

As much as Sam couldn't believe that she was in New York at one of her favorite conventions, she was more confused than ever. He couldn't have had this planned for long. "Matt, you have to have tickets for this. I think even the day passes have sold out."

"I know." He kissed her. A quick press of familiar lips, gone in a moment. Then her door was opened for her.

She got out, followed by Matt. While he spoke to Diego, Sam stared at the posters outside the venue. No wonder he'd insisted on her wearing her comfy shoes and worn jeans. If she'd known, though, she might have worn her Black Widow cosplay costume. She loved the character and didn't have to dye her hair. Then again, maybe she wouldn't have worn it. Not under the circumstances.

Matt's arm went around her shoulders. "You ready? We're meeting the liaison at the main entrance."

It was a quick walk filled with a lot of civilians and cosplayers. Phones were already in use, taking selfies for Instagram. A short slim woman who looked all business must have recognized Matt as they approached the doors.

"Mr. Wilkinson, I'm Grace Potter. Nice to meet you."

He shook her hand. "Thanks for going to so much trouble."

"It's our pleasure."

"May I introduce—"

"Oh, I know who you are," Grace said, turning to Sam. "It's a privilege to meet you, Ms. O'Connel. I play 'Tree Town' all the time. It's one of my favorite games. And the work you did on 'Red Velvet'? I just— I'm such an admirer. These passes are all access, including backstage at all our official venues. But I don't think you'll have trouble getting into any of our Super Week partner showcases. And here's my card. Anything you need, you call me. That's my personal number."

"Thank you." Sam blushed. "I'm really honored to get these passes. I promise we won't lose them." She put her lanyard over her neck and watched Matt do the same. He didn't seem upset that she was the center of attention, but then, he hadn't been like that ever. All she saw was his pride and respect for her.

"Shall we?" He held out his hand.

She took it, and it was like walking into Oz. It was only day one, so it didn't smell too much like spandex sweat yet. "You really are insane for bringing me here, but thank you," she said. "Have you ever been?"

"Nope." The noise, the hugeness of the place, made them both slow to a stop. "How do we navigate this?"

"We go up," she said. "That's the real treat in having passes like these. We can look out over the floor and plan our attack from there."

"You have some favorite things to do?"

"Oh, yes. If Diego's the one picking us up, I hope he brings a bigger car. I tend to spend a lot."

"No," he said, mocking her terribly.

"Well, most of the things I've collected are worth a lot of money now."

"Oh, so you plan on selling them?"

"Are you crazy?" she said and realized when he grinned how she'd really walked into that one.

He squeezed her hand. "It doesn't matter. As long as you get pleasure from it."

"Coming here with a virgin is pretty pleasurable."

"What? Oh. Yes. Is there an initiation or something?"

She wiggled her eyebrows, prepared to love every second of this. Of them. "We'll get to that later."

HIS ARM WAS getting sore. They'd made a bet that whoever saw a lemon in their travels got to hit the other in the arm. It was more of a token hit, but he'd spotted exactly two, whereas Sam had found eleven. He didn't even understand why they were looking for lemons. It had to do with some radio show, and very definitely something to do with geek culture.

They spent some quality time with actors and writers whose names even he recognized. Sam was a celebrity in her own right and handled those conversations like a pro. When they finally left the heady altitude of the all-access-pass realm, they walked the floor, arguing over which superhero from the Avengers was the best. He was squarely on the side of Captain America, but Sam was convinced it was Iron Man. It got pretty heated. It ended only when they got to her favorite shopping mall, Artist Alley.

The plan was to buy whatever took their fancy. And he was surprised to actually feel somewhat at home there. He'd become a minor collector of some of the comics Sam had turned him on to way back.

All the major franchises were represented in art, books and merchandise. *Star Wars*, *Doctor Who*, *Star Trek*, *Firefly*, Marvel, DC, *The Walking Dead*, *Game of Thrones*. The list was never ending.

But so was the fascination he felt watching Sam in this world. Lots of people knew who she was. At first he'd thought all the skeezy-looking guys were checking her out, but then he realized that they had probably seen her picture and were just trying to figure out if it was really her.

She'd been especially welcomed in the booths of the game companies she'd worked with. It was really something. They were so surprised to see her, and all those brilliant men and women treated her like royalty.

She'd stopped at a lot of booths, and the two very large tote bags he held were already filled. But now she was at a vendor's booth scoping out something that definitely wouldn't fit in a car.

"How much, including delivery?" she asked. "And what do I do? Just send you the dimensions and it replaces a regular door?"

The man nodded and Matt grinned. The guy made

doors that looked like the phone box from *Doctor Who*. Of course she would want one. It was perfect. If he'd seen it for sale somewhere, he'd have bought it for her himself.

The amount was a lot, as was the time needed to custom-make one and the cost to ship it to her. But the seller knew who Sam was and said he'd give her a discount if she'd let him have some pictures of her with the door after it had been installed.

She was glowing. Watching her have such a good time touched him deeply. She kept telling him who was dressed up like whom, stopping a lot of the women cosplayers to compliment them on their looks. It was charming as hell, especially when she got excited about questionable homemade costumes made with lots of love but little talent.

Sam was even more captivating here than she had been at the gala, and she'd impressed him beyond words there.

But the best part of the experience was when they were on the main exhibition floor, trying out games together. It didn't matter who was around or what anybody thought—they went all out. Or as Sam liked to say, "balls to the walls." He tried to argue that she was lacking in that department, but she just laughed and said, "Sweet Matthew, mine are big and brass and you'd better be careful because there's an ET who's about to eat your head."

By the time they left, he was exhausted. Hard-core fandom was something he could appreciate, but he was more than ready to have Sam all to himself. They got to his place just after 10:00 p.m. It felt great to be home. To share it with Sam. He ordered a pizza, and they took showers—separately, to his chagrin—but it didn't really matter. Because when he came out of the steamy bathroom, there she was in a nightshirt sitting on his bed, a big smile on her face. She looked so beautiful it made his heart stutter.

And she was his. At least for now. And he was pretty sure his odds of convincing her they could make it together had shot up.

SAM PUT HER chin on her fist and had herself a good old-fashioned ogle. "You're so hot when you just come out of the shower wearing a teeny towel around your waist."

"Thanks. I like your outfit, too."

"Ah, you're just saying that 'cause you're horny."

"Not true." He tossed the towel in the corner. He wasn't exactly hard as a rock, but he was getting there. "'Horny' indicates something vague, as if any woman could satisfy me, when I only want you."

She smiled as he crawled into bed beside her. His hair still damp, he laid his head on his pillow, his eyes already darkened by desire. His minty breath brushed across her lips and slipped into her mouth.

"Tell me something," she said. "How did you come up with this plan?"

His hand reached her before his words, and he slid his palm all the way from her neck down past her bottom and then made the return journey. "I promise to tell you, but later."

Sam held on to a smile. She had no doubt the sex would be good. Off the charts. But she wondered if it was wrong to lead him on. She wasn't sure what he'd been trying to prove by bringing her to New York or Comic Con, because it still changed nothing about their situation.

No, it wasn't wrong for them to enjoy each other. That was the main reason she'd come. To be with Matt.

"What are you waiting for?" she asked with a teasing smile.

He moved the last few inches until his lips were so close to hers they breathed the same breath. From deep in his throat came a husky masculine sound that did something wicked to her insides. After removing her nightshirt, he ran his hands across every inch of her, as if he wanted to memorize every part of her body. She found herself doing the same thing—rubbing his hard muscles under his smooth, clean skin, reveling in the brush of his soft chest hair. Somewhere along the way, her leg had moved over his hip and she could feel the press of his very hard erection against her thigh.

"Condom," he said. "Don't move."

She nodded, but then he knocked her leg down as he rolled to open his side-table drawer. She laughed, but he was back in a flash. As soon as he'd put on the damn thing, he lifted her leg back to his hip.

Then he kissed the stuffing out of her.

When she caught her breath again, he cupped her chin with his hand. "Hey. We can do something fancy next time, okay? This time, let's just—"

She nodded eagerly and he was suddenly over her, making himself comfortable between her thighs. She felt him tremble. This strong, singular man was literally shaking with desire.

She lifted her hips, and he didn't waste a second, quickly sliding a pillow under her.

"I hated being away from you," he said, his voice three steps up from a growl. "I'm so goddamn glad you're here."

He entered her in one smooth glide, making her moan. No one else had ever made her feel this way. He seemed to be the key that unlocked all of her passion.

For a moment, the reality of their inevitable end made her gasp, but she shoved the thoughts away.

He didn't even try to slow his pace once he looked at her. His face was right above hers, his back arched, sturdy arms holding him up. He found their connection, the one that had never been severed, and together, they moved as if they were made for this. For each other. The sex wasn't all that fast, but it grew more intense by the minute. His thumb brought her off right before he lost his control and came inside her. There was a long note of tension, stretching so thin it had to break. When it did, he flopped beside her. Her insides twitched a few times, as did his legs, but the electricity between them continued to spark as they tried to get their breathing under control.

Finally, he ran his free hand over her cheek, his fingers tunneling into her hair, holding her steady. "Did you have fun today?"

A lump rose in her throat. God, she hoped this wasn't his big plan. "You know I did."

"I had fun, too."

"Not as much as I did."

He laughed. "Probably not."

"Thank you, Matthew. I know you must have gone through a lot of trouble. I don't even know how you managed to get tickets at the last minute. I'm assuming this was a spur-of-the-moment plan?"

He nodded. "But it wasn't any trouble at all." His eyes bored into hers. "Explain something to me. You love this stuff so much, why didn't you book tickets?"

It amazed her that Matt, of all people, just couldn't

seem to understand her schedule. She sighed and pulled away. "I'm serious," he said. "And puzzled. How long has it been since you've come to one of these?"

"Matt, please. I shouldn't have to explain this. I could barely eke out time for you. You know how busy I am."

"I do," he said, nodding. "And yet here you are. For three whole days."

She started to say something but closed her mouth and stared at him instead.

"When I said it wasn't any trouble getting into the convention, I wasn't kidding."

"Well, yeah." She gave a casual shrug, but the unease in her chest hadn't diminished. "I realized after I said it, with your name and resources, you could probably get anything you—"

"I had little to do with it. I just used your name and—" He snapped his fingers.

"What?" Sam let out a nervous laugh. "My name?"

"Yes, your name, Ms. O'Connel. They were very happy to accommodate the genius behind 'Tree Town' and all the security programs you've designed." Matt smiled and moved closer to her. "Look, Sam, anything that happened today, starting with the first-class plane ride, the car picking us up, tickets to the convention… You have the resources to get all those things for yourself. But apparently, you needed me to do it for you." He leaned closer and kissed her gently. "Just like I need you to remind me life isn't only about work."

He ran the backs of his fingers down her cheek. "I don't remember having a better time than I did with you over this past week. I felt like a kid again. And I know you did, too. God, watching you today… What's wrong with making time for fun? For each other? Life is brimming with possibilities, my beautiful Sammy. Are we going to ignore them? I'm not saying our careers aren't important. I love what I do, and I'm going to continue to do it for as long as possible. But I'm very clear that I love you more. And years from now I don't want to look back at my life and see that I missed out on the most important things. We balance each other out, Sam. We do. You can't deny that."

Right now she couldn't do much of anything. Except blink back tears. "Damn you, Matt."

"Is that a good 'damn you' or a—" He laughed and caught her hand when she tried to smack him. Then he kissed each of her fingertips.

Sam knew she should say something. But there was so much new data flashing in her brain that she couldn't gather her wits.

"Sometimes you'll come with me to a gala," he said, "and sometimes I'll go with you to a con. We'll still both work too much, but maybe not as much as we have been."

"And here I just learned how to be a grown-up." She kissed his lower lip, then took it between her teeth and gave it a gentle tug. But then she let him go, her eyes widening. "Wait. Did you say you love me?"

He smiled. "Sweetheart, remember when I asked if work was all you loved? It wasn't rhetorical. Of course I love you. Very much. I've never been more sure of anything. I know that in the beginning I'll need to travel more than I'd like to, but I can start taking a more supervisory approach to our acquisitions. I also happen to know that I'll be able to make my home base Boston. I'd keep this place so we could visit and because we both love the city. We could stretch out our obligations bit by bit. Maybe hire a personal assistant or two? Have date nights, play 'House of the Dead' until I can just win one damn game. And be together at the end of the day."

Sam's heart was beating so hard she thought it might burst out of her chest. It was all she could do to say, "I'm overwhelmed. You did all this, turning down the promotion, arranging this vivid illustration of your point, for me?"

He shook his head in the kindest way. "I'm good at what I do. I'll get where I want to go. It'll be so much easier when I have a partner at home. But there's still one thing I'm not sure of."

"What's that?"

"If you love me back."

She knocked him over in her eagerness to kiss him. "Of course I love you," she said between kisses. "And this plan. This 'carpe diem' life you're talking about, I want that. I want to have more than my work. I just never had a better offer."

"Then I'm yours. For as long as you'll have me."

"Oh, my God. This is the best thing that's ever happened in the history of ever."

He laughed, but she was completely serious. "Tomorrow you should go to the con as a superhero."

He looked at her as his brows rose. "A superhero? Which one?"

The only one that mattered. "Matthew Wilkinson."

* * * * *

COMING NEXT MONTH FROM

HARLEQUIN *Blaze*

Available April 19, 2016

#891 DARING HER SEAL
Uniformly Hot!
by Anne Marsh
DEA agent Ashley Dixon and Navy SEAL Levi Brandon are
shocked to discover their faux wedding from their last mission
was legitimate. They don't even like each other! Which doesn't
mean they aren't hot for each other...

#892 COME CLOSER, COWBOY
Made in Montana
by Debbi Rawlins
Hollywood transplant Mallory Brandt is opening a new bar in
Blackfoot Falls. She needs a fresh start, but sexy stuntman
Gunner Ellison is determined to remind her of the past...one
amazing night in particular.

#893 BIG SKY SEDUCTION
by Daire St. Denis
When uptight Gloria Hurst sleeps with laid-back cowboy
Dillon Cross, she does what any control freak would do—pretend
it never happened. But a moment of weakness is quickly turning
into something that could last a lifetime!

#894 THE FLYBOY'S TEMPTATION
by Kimberly Van Meter
Former Air Force pilot J.T. Carmichael knew Dr. Hope Larsen's
request to fly into the Mexican jungle came with a mess of
complications. But when they're stranded, the heat between
them becomes too hard to resist...

**YOU CAN FIND MORE INFORMATION ON UPCOMING HARLEQUIN® TITLES,
FREE EXCERPTS AND MORE AT WWW.HARLEQUIN.COM.**

HBCNM0416

SPECIAL EXCERPT FROM

HARLEQUIN Blaze

*Terminal bachelor and Navy SEAL Levi Brandon
finds himself accidentally married to Ashley Dixon,
a DEA agent who definitely doesn't like him...though
sparks seem to fly whenever they're together!*

Read on for a sneak preview of
DARING HER SEAL, by New York Times
bestselling author Anne Marsh,
part of Harlequin Blaze's
UNIFORMLY HOT! miniseries.

"Can you be married without having sex?"

Levi Brandon's SEAL team leader, Gray Jackson,
slapped him on the back, harder than was strictly
necessary. "Last time I checked, you weren't married,
planning on getting married or even dating the same
woman for consecutive nights. The better question is...
can you go without having sex?"

He'd tried dating when he was younger. Hell. The word
younger made him feel like Methuselah, but the feeling
wasn't inaccurate. Courtesy of Uncle Sam, he'd seen
plenty and done more. The civilian women he'd dated once
upon a time didn't understand what his job entailed.

He certainly had no plans for celibacy. On the other
hand, fate had just slapped him with the moral equivalent
of a chastity belt. Levi pulled the marriage certificate out
of a pocket of his flight suit and waved it at his team.

Sam unfolded the paper, read it over and whistled.
"You're married?"

"Not on purpose," Levi admitted with a scowl.

Mason held out a hand for the certificate. "When did this happen?"

"I'm blaming you." Mason was a big bear of a SEAL, a damned good sniper and the second member of their unit to find *true love* when they'd been undercover on Fantasy Island three months ago. "Your girl asked Ashley and me to be the stand-in bride and groom for a beach ceremony. She didn't tell us we were getting married for real."

Mason grinned. "Heads up. Every photo shoot with that woman is an adventure."

"Yeah," he grumbled, "but can you really imagine me married? To *Ashley*?"

Ashley Dixon had been a DEA tagalong on their past two missions. As far as he could tell, she disliked everything about him—she'd been happy to detail her opinions loudly and at length. Naturally he'd given her plenty of shit while they'd been in their field together, and she'd *really* hated him calling her Mrs. Brandon after they'd played bride and groom for Mason's girl.

After they'd parted ways on Fantasy Island, he hadn't thought of her once. Okay. He'd thought of her once. Maybe twice. She was gorgeous, they had a little history together and he wasn't dead yet, although he was fairly certain he *would* be if he pursued her. But how the hell had he ended up married to her?

*Don't miss DARING HER SEAL
by* New York Times *bestselling author Anne Marsh,
available May 2016 wherever
Harlequin® Blaze® books and ebooks are sold.*

www.Harlequin.com

HBEXP0416

Reading Has Its Rewards

Earn FREE BOOKS!

Register at **Harlequin My Rewards** and submit your Harlequin purchases from wherever you shop to earn points for free books and other exclusive rewards.

Plus submit your purchases from now till May 30th for a chance to win a $500 Visa Card*.

Visit **HarlequinMyRewards.com** today

MYR16R1

Looking for more passionate reads?
Collect these stories from
Harlequin Presents and Harlequin Desire!

HARLEQUIN *Presents.*

MORELLI'S MISTRESS
by *USA TODAY* bestselling author Anne Mather

Luke Morelli is back and determined that Abby Laurence
will pay for her past betrayal. Finally free of her husband,
there's only one way she can make amends… Their affair
was once illicit, but she's Luke's for the taking now!

HARLEQUIN *Desire*

TWINS FOR THE TEXAN
(Billionaires and Babies)
by *USA TODAY* bestselling author Charlene Sands

When Brooke McKay becomes pregnant after a one-night
stand with a sexy rancher, she tracks him down…only to
discover he's a widower struggling with toddler twins!
Can she help as his nanny before falling in love—and
delivering her baby bombshell?

Available wherever books and ebooks are sold.